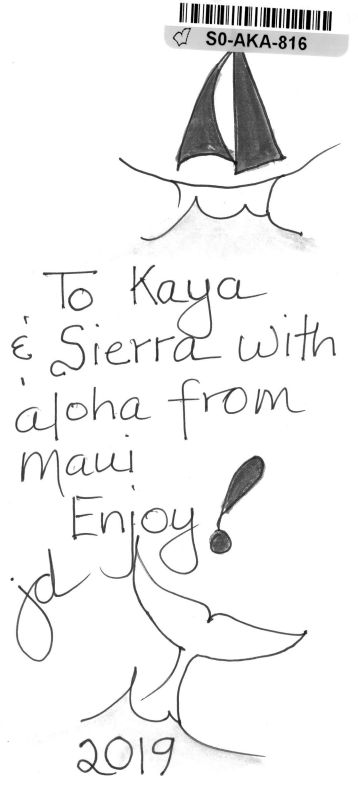

To Kaya
& Sierra with
ʻaloha from
maui
Enjoy!
jd

2019

JOHANN SEBASTIAN HUMPBACH

Jamie David

CHAI YO
MAUI PRESS

CHAI YO
MAUI PRESS

ISBN 978-0-615-31840-0

Library of Congress Control Number: 209909195

Cover illustration and chapter drawings by the author.

Cover design by Kathryn E. Campbell

Text Design by Patricia Coppedge

Printed in the U.S.A.

For Hawaii's keiki
and those who read to them

Float through it.

—Johann

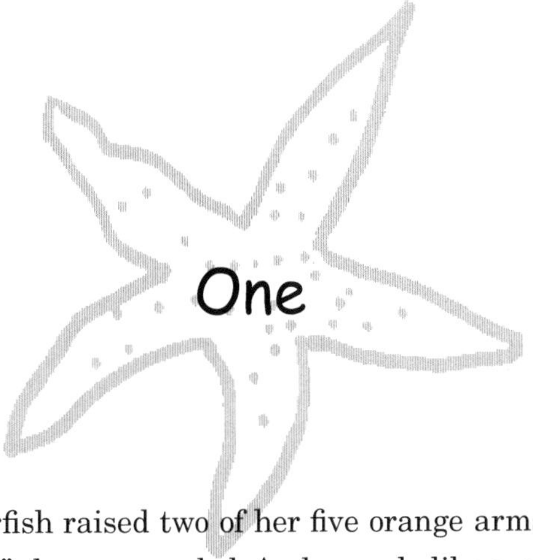

One

Venus Starfish raised two of her five orange arms. “Okay, girls, hit it!” she commanded. And swoosh, like a mermaid’s tail, thousands of fish darted into place. The Alaskan sun lit the flickering display and J-O-H-A-N-N floated across the sea in a shimmering water ballet.

Known around the world as the *Pavarotti* of whales for his beautiful tenor voice, Johann Sebastian Humpbach would soon be leaving these winter seas. His birthplace, Hawaii, called once again.

Bears and eagles, otters and seals, predatory orcas on good behavior all lined the rocky shore to see Johann off. It would be six months before he returned with tales of his Whale Song Tour. His friends and admirers longed to hear him sing, but Johann and his humpback clan only sang when they were in Hawaii.

Though he was already experiencing slight pangs of homesickness, Johann knew the feeling wouldn’t last for long. Thoughts of playing in warm Hawaii waters and performing for the multitudes filled Johann with warmth like the Hawaiian sun. There was nothing Johann loved more than singing his head off. To him it was pure happiness.

Next to singing, breaching was most dear to Johann's heart. In a show of strength and joy he parted the waves with a slap of his tail. The surrounding throngs went wild, cheering him on like fans at a soccer match. He felt powerful because he had bulked up on his favorite food, krill, all summer.

Johann was big, fat, and bursting at the seams. He was ready to go.

The gathering grew louder and louder, the cries and wishes bittersweet.

"Farewell, Johann."

"Make us proud, Johann."

"Have a great trip."

"Be safe."

"Bring back a CD."

Johann was deeply touched by the outpouring of affection. "Thank you, thank you," he said in his melodious voice, and it sounded like singing.

Then, he was off.

The way to the Hawaiian Islands was well known to this plucky traveler. Once en route Johann was grateful for the solitude, especially after all the hoopla surrounding his departure.

He glided along, invigorated by the chilly water yet welcoming warmer seas as he headed south. He encountered familiar faces along the way and enjoyed brief visits with old pals from journeys past. He made the 3,500-mile trip in good time, just under eighty-two days.

In waters off the Big Island of Hawaii Johann put on a show for a passing cruise ship, breaking the waves in full view of the delighted passengers. “Look, look,” they cried. Johann appeared on one side of the vessel and then the other. He watched from the corner of his eye as people scurried back and forth on the deck like sand crabs on the beach.

Things continued to go swimmingly and Johann, comfortable with his thoughts, settled once again into a steady rhythm . . . until, that is, the water turned a deep, dark purple.

Hmm, that’s an odd color for the sea to be, thought Johann. No sooner had the notion crossed his mind than an even stranger thing happened. Johann began to grow drowsy. His eyelids were heavy lead weights. His once clear thoughts became muddy as they gradually slipped away.

Two

"No way."

"I don't want to dress like you either, Keoni," said Leilani.

Auntie Pua sighed. "It was just a suggestion. It's your birthday. You'd look so cute, *yeah*, just like when you were little."

"Auntie, we haven't dressed alike since we were four," protested Leilani, "and besides, we'd look like tourists."

"Fine, but we don't have all day. I've got a million and one things to do for tonight."

"Lei! Rock-scissors-paper!" challenged Keoni.

"Ready—set—go!" Leilani replied. Her clenched fist shot out from behind her back and flattened out, fingers spread. "Paper covers rock. I win, *Brah*! Tough luck."

Leilani was triumphant as she slipped on the red and yellow hibiscus print aloha shirt they both had their eyes on, available in boys' and girls' styles. "This looks *really* cool on me, better than it would on you," she said, pleased with her reflection in the store mirror. She liked her new haircut too. Shoulder-length suited her more now, better than the waist-length hair she had worn before.

"No problem . . . I'll find something else. Anything's better than looking like you," said Keoni. He laughed as he dodged a punch that landed mid-air.

"Okay, you guys. Cool it," said Auntie Pua, and that was that.

Three

Johann woke slowly as if from a twenty-year sleep. His temples throbbed. Was this a headache? He'd heard of headaches before but he'd never had one personally.

Like a scrawny stagehand trying to raise a heavy curtain, Johann struggled to open his eyes. Little by little he realized he was in trouble. He was in an unknown place with zero visibility. For the first time in his life Johann trembled.

One minute he was basking in warm Hawaiian waters and now, this. "Don't panic," he told himself. "Be strong." He struggled to recover his courage as he found himself on the edge of fear.

A piercing cold filled the darkness. Johann couldn't stop shivering. An enormous chill crawled from the tip of his tail flukes to the crown of his head. Then it began all over again, creeping up his spine. Was he dying? He was confused and he knew it, so he began to sing.

Johann's voice was weak and cracked at first, but he kept on. "Do, re, mi, fa, sol, la, ti, do . . . do, ti, la, sol, fa, mi, re, do," he warbled, and felt better.

As his thoughts cleared he could have sworn he heard laughter. Not happy. Not joyous. But an eerie kind of laughter. Was his mind playing tricks on him? There it was again. He could hear it clearly in the deep, dark depths. Then it drifted away.

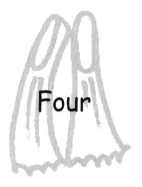

Four

A necklace of stars glittered above while the inviting sounds of Hawaiian slack-key guitar filled Auntie Pua and Uncle Kalani's backyard. The twins and their friends swayed to the music like adolescent palm trees brushed by gentle trade winds.

"Uncle Kawika's trio is awesome," Keoni said proudly to his friends. "We're lucky, you know, 'cuz— "

"—They play at the Ritz Carlton Hotel," said Leilani, finishing Keoni's sentence. "They're called *Nalu*. Cool name, huh? It means wave."

The squeaking of the backyard gate alerted them to a new arrival. "Uncle Oliver's here, Uncle Oliver's here!" they shouted. Aunties, uncles, cousins, and friends rushed to greet the white-haired *kupuna*.

"What'cha got in the basket, Uncle?" teased Keoni. He knew from past experience the beloved elder would bring them *opihi*, the Hawaiian delicacy gathered from wave-washed rocks. Picking the little shellfish could be a dangerous pastime. Many an *opihi* picker had been swept away by a rogue wave, never to be seen again.

"I can see'm now, roasting on *kiawe* coals with Auntie's homemade salsa," said Keoni rubbing his tummy. "Nice 'n spicy."

"You better not eat any, *Brah*. That *opu's* goin' get fat!" said Leilani, laughing and pointing at Keoni's slender stomach.

"C'mon, everybody, dig in," called out Auntie Pua in a cheery, sing song voice. She sank a bamboo paddle into a large pot of fluffy steamed rice. Keoni helped his Uncle Kalani carry a large *koa* "pig board" laden with the *imu*-baked *kalua* pig to the picnic table decorated with pineapples and papayas, *ti* leaves and ferns.

In this land of hearty appetites the guests surrounded the feast like hungry fish on a coral reef. Auntie Pua's *poi* didn't last long, disappearing as fast as ice cubes in the sun.

With full *opu* straining against the waistband of their shorts, the musicians sauntered back to the stage of plywood and cement blocks, "*Ey*, Auntie Pua, you and your girls come up here," coaxed Uncle Kawika, motioning towards the platform with chubby fingers and strumming his guitar with the other hand. A little good-natured urging, and the women made their way to the stage.

How pretty Auntie Pua looked when she wore orchids in her wavy, salt and pepper hair, thought Leilani. In vibrant Hawaiian print *muumuu* and fragrant plumeria *lei* Auntie and her daughters looked like the dancers on glossy travel brochures as they performed their favorite hulas. "*Hana hou, hana hou*" chanted the partygoers, not stopping until they were treated to an encore.

As the twins were being serenaded by a rowdy version

of "Happy Birthday to You," a glowing birthday cake magically appeared before them. Auntie Pua made a yellow layer for Leilani and a chocolate layer for Keoni with creamy coconut *haupia* in between. Making silent wishes, the twins extinguished twelve tiny flames with one mingled breath. Wishes made now would surely come true.

Their presents from Auntie Pua and Uncle Kalani were wrapped in the Sunday comics and tied with gold and silver ribbon, hinting at the fun they held inside. "Cooool!" said Keoni at the sight of a new mask, fins and snorkel. His grin was so wide, it made his dark eyes disappear.

Please, please, let me get dive gear too, thought Leilani. She was not to be disappointed. Her gear was just like Keoni's except for the color, a bright, sunny yellow instead of a soft, sky-blue like her brother's.

There was one more gift from their auntie and uncle, a gift for the two of them, to be shared.

Five

Auntie Pua was relaxing for the first time that busy day. A few curls had escaped from her pulled-back hair, framing her smiling round face. Though she was a little plumper now, Auntie Pua had an ageless quality, with smooth unlined skin. She seemed to advance from one decade to the next, barely changed. With her hands resting in her lap and her legs crossed at the ankles, she looked as contented as a queen. She watched expectantly as Keoni tore the gift wrap off a box dotted with stickers of humpback whales.

"Go ahead, Lei, you open it," said Keoni, handing his sister the box.

"You know, sometimes they really can be sweet to each other . . . " Auntie Pua whispered to her husband Uncle Kalani who was sitting next to her.

Leilani lifted the lid and folded back the crisp white tissue. "Cooool," chorused the twins as they high-fived at the sight of shiny black binoculars.

There was one more thing in the box, a white envelope sealed with a breaching whale sticker. "Your turn, *Brah*," said Leilani, handing Keoni the envelope.

"Wow!" marveled the twins. "Two tickets to Johann Sebastian Humpbach's Whale Song Tour on the *Hana Hou!* Thank you, Auntie and Uncle. *Mahalo!*"

Six

Captain Kenny was comfortably seated in his new leather office chair, a gift from his employees. "Things are looking up," he muttered to Noe his long time assistant as he looked over the passenger roster for the next snorkel trip on the *Hana Hou*.

It had been a tough year in the boating business, though Captain Kenny had been luckier than most when the big storm hit. His prized sailboat, the *Hana Hou* had been in dry-dock at the time and sustained little damage, unlike the boats of less fortunate friends.

Still, he had a lot riding on the upcoming winter whale watch season. "It's make-it or break-it time," said the captain. "Heck, the whale watches are as important to the boating business as Christmas is to retail."

He was glad he had decided to expand his business by selling souvenirs on board. The custom designed T-shirts for the Johann Sebastian Humpbach Whale Song Tour had been ordered. Johann was coming to the islands and tickets were nearly sold out.

"Yesiree," Captain Kenny marveled, "that Johann keeps

getting better and better. And it's not just the tourists, local people love him too." The captain hoped to carry CDs of Johann's music before long. A recording session was scheduled for mid-January.

Captain Kenny didn't think of himself as being exploitive. He was simply sharing Johann's gifts and making a little money in the process. Nothing wrong with that.

Seven

Mr. Witherspoon was in a bit of a tizzy. "Tsk, tsk," he fretted. As a perfectionist and the supervisor in charge, he worried about the length of the *kukui nut lei* his volunteers were making for Johann.

"The *kukui* nuts must be gathered, cleaned, polished, drilled and strung," he lectured. Considering Johann's considerable girth, this was no small task. Mr. Witherspoon's staff was up to the challenge and went about its business despite his hand ringing and anxious looks.

"Don't take it personally," they said to each other, "that's just Witherspoon."

The *kukui nut lei* had been his wife's idea and was so well received by Johann and his public that it was becoming a tradition. Johann was relieved to shed the famous wool scarf he wore while in Alaska and replace it with something from Hawaii. Truth be told, Johann was not opposed to a bit of adornment now and then.

"We have the honor of sailing on the lead boat and presenting our esteemed guest with the giant *lei*," Mr. Witherspoon proudly informed his wife.

“That’s as it should be, dear,” said Mrs. Witherspoon returning to her lecture on Johann. She had snared a group of tourists outside her office in the old missionary-era museum building and wasn’t about to let them get away.

“Since Johann is a scout, he will be preceding his fellow humpbacks by weeks or even months. Perhaps this custom stems from the old whaling days when humpbacks were prized prey. Now that whaling in Hawaiian waters is a relic of the past, the pilot’s role is viewed by some as largely ceremonial,” she continued without pausing to take a breath. “But they are mistaken. Humpbacks may no longer be the target of a whaler’s harpoon, but hazards still abound. Pollution can make them sick, and acoustic disturbances can cause them pain. Collisions with ships are deadly, and entanglement in marine debris can spell the end.

“To the rest of the world Johann may be a celebrity but to the endangered humpbacks he is their pilot whale. They have entrusted Johann with the position as pilot for as long as he desires. Like all great leaders, he has earned their trust!”

Needless to say, Mr. Witherspoon’s able wife Clara, and not he, was in charge of Johann’s welcoming festivities. It was she who coordinated the events surrounding the flotilla. Colorful bunting would adorn the masts of boats from the humble to the grand. Hula dancers and a variety of bands were set to entertain the festive crowds down near the harbor. Charitable groups would man their fund-raising food booths under the ancient Banyan tree by the old courthouse. Traffic control, permits for souvenir sellers and countless other details needed attending to.

Clara Witherspoon handled it all with efficiency and confidence. She was in her element. She was large and in charge.

Eight

The twins were already at the window of the *shave ice* stand before Uncle Kalani could even lock his Toyota pickup. Their birthday-day was turning into birthday-week. Their auntie and uncle were treating them to a day at their favorite beach.

"Blueberry-banana, please," ordered Keoni.

"Pineapple-mango for me," added Leilani, not missing a beat.

The *shave ice* refreshed them as they followed the well-worn path to the beach through the *kiawe* forest. It was idyllic as a fairy tale with dappled light sifting through the trees. Keoni and Leilani skipped along.

"Look, a mongoose!" Leilani exclaimed, pointing to the creature as it darted into the brush. A pair of cardinals appeared, one a bright red male and the other a gray female, flying down the trail before the twins, their ushers for the day.

At the end of the path the shade of the forest gave way to the blazing sun of the beach. It was like coming out of a dark movie theater on a sunny day.

"Not many people here," said Leilani, "more room for us."

"Yeah. And the water's nice 'n flat," said Keoni.

This was the first outing for their new snorkel gear. Keoni and Leilani were already accomplished snorkelers and though respectful of the awesome power of the sea were not fearful of it. Auntie Pua called them the "Tuna Twins" because they were so at home in the water. If past experience was any indication, they would spend little time on the beach, dashing into the water at the first opportunity and staying there until it was time for lunch.

Uncle Kalani was a strong swimmer and diver and always accompanied the twins when they swam out to the reef to snorkel. He would often say, "Remember you two, this is the open ocean, not a swimming pool."

Auntie Pua wasn't much into snorkeling. She said, "I think I'll hang out here. Maybe just bounce around in the water when it gets too hot. I'm gonna sit in my beach chair and read my magazine. You guys go have fun."

Leilani was the first one in the water after they had all helped Auntie Pua set up camp for the day. Auntie Pua signaled with a *shaka* as Keoni and Uncle Kalani followed Leilani into the waves.

They didn't stray far from one another, knowing the first rule of water safety was to stay together. Besides, it was always more fun to share an adventure. Once Leilani was swimming next to what she thought was a large rock. Keoni thought it was a rock too. Turns out it was a *honu*, a green sea turtle. "Shoots, fooled us both," said Keoni.

In one spot five *honu* lay motionless on the bottom of the ocean. "Hey, guys! Over there!" shouted Leilani, pointing excitedly at the ancient looking reptiles. With their leathery skin and bony shells they reminded Leilani of the old men who hung out in the shopping center courtyard, playing checkers under the monkey pod trees.

"Some fish are so funny looking. I like trumpet fish the best. They really look like trumpets, *yeah*?" said Leilani, blowing salty water from her nostrils.

Keoni free-dived to about fifteen feet as he followed a large rainbow-colored parrotfish through trees of coral. The fish disappeared at the entrance to an underwater lava cave where Keoni swam in a circle looking for his elusive playmate. As he spun around he saw what all snorkelers hope for—to see something they've never seen before.

The thing was billowy with thread-like tentacles. Keoni wanted to explore further but was almost out of breath. He surfaced, emerging a few feet away from Leilani, who was treading water. Her mask was resting on the back of her head.

"What was that, Keoni? I saw something weird."

"Me too. Let's check it out."

Leilani readjusted her mask and she and Keoni dove toward the undulating shape near the entrance to the cave.

Upon closer inspection the twins realized that the creature before them was not a creature at all. The thing was snagged on the sharp lava rock and rolled back and forth in the surge like a flag in the wind. Leilani nodded to Keoni and he freed one of its ends. She undid the other, prying it from the grasping crevice. Leilani gave her brother a thumbs-up and they both headed for the surface, their find in tow.

Nine

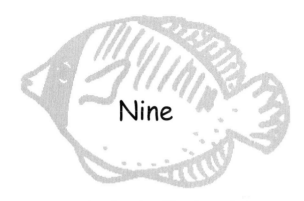

Captain Kenny made a decision. The channel was too rough that day to make the snorkel trip to Lanai as planned. Determined not to disappoint his passengers, he would take them somewhere equally impressive.

The *Hana Hou* headed toward the south shore, to a destination beyond the string of deluxe resorts that looked like gleaming palaces when viewed from the sea. Captain Kenny knew a reef that promised not only coral and tropical fish but green sea turtles too. He scanned the horizon with his spyglass hoping to see the waterspout of a humpback whale.

His cell phone vibrated in his pocket. *It's probably Noe*, he thought.

"Aloha, Captain Kenny here."

"Captain, you're gonna kill me. I couldn't help it. She was so . . . so insistent."

"Who? What are you talking about?"

"Mrs. Witherspoon, Clara Witherspoon. She wouldn't give up until I gave her your cell phone number. She said you hadn't returned her calls and she had something urgent she had to discuss with you. Sorry, boss. You know how she is."

"Geez, Noe . . . okay, okay." said Captain Kenny, looking none too happy.

He was not in the mood to talk to Clara Witherspoon. He suspected she had thought of one more thing for him to do for the Johann festivities. Not that the captain begrudged Johann his due. Lord knows he had as much to gain as anyone.

Captain Kenny was happy to help Mrs. Witherspoon, to a point. But plans were growing more and more elaborate each day, and he already had his hands full.

But Mrs. Witherspoon had not called to cajole him into doing one more task. She didn't make the slightest attempt to *talk story* or engage in the usual pleasantries.

"Captain, I'm worried," she blurted out. "Johann should have been spotted by now. Research vessels usually cross paths with him when he's close by. The crews alert us of his ETA."

"Don't get all up-in-arms, Clara. He could have gotten off to a late start, or run into friends or even decided to travel a different route. Johann can take care of himself."

"I don't have a good feeling about this, not at all, not at all," she said, her voice rising. "Perhaps I could go for a sail with you on the *Hana Hou* and we could have a look for ourselves."

Oh, great, thought the captain.

"Clara, I'm sure he's fine. Look, I've got a business to

run. The *Hana Hou* is fully booked. I can't cancel the trips and disappoint the customers. What kind of *aloha* would that be? Besides, I need the money," he said in a hushed voice. He didn't want anyone on board to be privy to his finances, not even his loyal first mate Charlie who was in earshot.

"You're probably right, Captain," said Mrs. Witherspoon, though she sounded uncertain.

Captain Kenny hung up the phone and gazed at the horizon. He took off his sunglasses, rubbed his eyes and the deep furrow between them.

"What's up, Captain?" Charlie asked, thinking the captain suddenly looked tired and worried.

"Nothing, Charlie . . . *nada* . . ." the captain said, his voice trailing off.

The crew carefully anchored the *Hana Hou,* so as not to damage the coral reef that had formed on a finger of lava about five hundred yards from the beach. With the crew assisting the novices, the snorkelers put on their gear. They were receiving the last of their instructions when a snorkel, and then a head, popped up in the water next to the anchored boat.

"*Aloha,*" called out Uncle Kalani, surprising the passengers and crew with his appearance in the middle of nowhere.

Captain Kenny rushed toward the boat's rail and returned the greeting in a booming voice, "*Ey, aloha* to you too, *Brah.*" He and Uncle Kalani had known each other for years, since high school when Captain Kenny had been best friends with Uncle Kalani's older brother Kawika.

Leilani and Keoni surfaced next to their uncle, still

clutching the object they had found clinging to the rocks below. "What'cha got there, kids?" Charlie asked.

"Don't know," responded Keoni, "can we come on board and check it out?"

Charlie lowered a rope ladder over the side. Dragging along their dripping find, Uncle Kalani and the twins climbed up the ladder and onto the gleaming teakwood deck.

Ten

The *Hana Hou's* passengers were as eager as children in an amusement park to explore the wonderland below. The snorkelers slipped into the cobalt blue water, barely taking notice of the twins and their prize.

Captain Kenny grinned from ear to ear at the unexpected reunion with his boyhood friend Kalani. "*Ey*, Kalani, you still have all that hair," said the captain, "and with Pua's *ono grinds*, why aren't you fat by now, *Brah*?" They embraced in one of those short, manly hugs that end with a pat on the back. Life had been busy and they hadn't seen each other since Uncle Kawika's Christmas party a couple of years ago.

"Kids, this is the Captain Kenny you've heard so much about," said Uncle Kalani, proudly introducing Keoni and Leilani to the captain. Captain Kenny, though not a tall man, looked robust and sturdy. His face was tan and leathery, with deep crow's-feet spreading from the corners of his eyes. His sunglasses hung from a cord around his neck and a baseball cap hid his thinning brown hair.

To Captain Kenny the twins seemed spirited and smart,

what the Hawaiians called *akamai. They look so much like Malia,* he thought, fixing his gaze on their tawny, wet faces. Two broad smiles beamed back at him, and something familiar twinkled in their dark, almond-shaped eyes. Keoni and Leilani were built like their late mother too, long-legged and athletic. Malia had been a volleyball star, so different from her sister Pua who spent most of her time in the kitchen.

"I hear you'll be joining us for Johann Sebastian Humpbach's Whale Song Tour," said the captain. "We're gonna have one good time."

Everyone forgot about Keoni and Leilani's discovery while they *talked story,* chatting about this and that, catching up, telling tales. It was Charlie who was first to express interest in the twin's found object. "What the heck is that anyway?" he asked.

It covered the length of the deck when unfurled. Everyone got down on hands and knees to better examine what, at first glance, looked like an expanse of nighttime sky. The color was midnight blue, the material a delicate wool appliquéd all over with twinkling stars in silver and gold. The stitching was so fine it could only have been done by hand.

"It's so soft and fluffy," marveled Leilani as she rubbed the woven cloth on her cheek, "like rabbit fur." The metallic stars glistened so brightly in the morning sun they seemed to dance.

"*Shoots*, under water I thought those were tentacles," said Keoni of the silky fringe made of silver and gold.

Uncle Kalani exclaimed, "This is impossible! It's completely dry!"

"You're right," said the captain. "Just feel it!"

Leilani had been so caught up in touching the cashmere-like softness that the fact it was dry hadn't occurred to her before. It appeared as though it just emerged from a giant Macy's gift box, instead of from the sea.

"Look at this!" she shouted, her eyes widening in surprised recognition as she stroked the silky fringe. There before them on the cloth, in glimmering threads of silver and gold, were embroidered the initials JSH.

Eleven

From her vantage point on the beach Auntie Pua looked up from her reading and saw a sailboat anchored in the distance. *This is a little bit of heaven*, she mused, *so peaceful and quiet*. Only the rhythmic sound of breaking waves and an occasional chirping bird on the edge of the forest punctuated the stillness.

A *lei* of clouds hovering over the mountain rolled into the path of the fiery sun, cooling everything below. Its timing was perfect. Just when it got too hot, the friendly vapor would mute the streaming rays that blazed through the sky.

Auntie Pua enjoyed burrowing her feet in the warm beige sand and leaned forward in her beach chair, the pages of the magazine on her lap fluttering in the breeze. She scanned the distance looking for Leilani's bright yellow snorkel. There was no sign of the Tuna Twins or their uncle. *They must be on the other side of the point*, she thought, wishing that they had brought along the twins' new binoculars after all. It was she who had vetoed bringing them to the beach. She hadn't wanted to expose them to wind, water and sand so fine it got into everything, even places you didn't know you had.

Auntie Pua put her sunglasses back on and returned to her reading, an intriguing story about a former White House chef.

The peaceful morning was interrupted by the familiar and yet bothersome ring of her cell phone. Auntie Pua fumbled around in her beach bag, feeling for the phone that was buried beneath colorful towels. For a moment she was tempted to ignore it. Then she thought of her oldest daughter Uilani whose baby was due in two weeks. Auntie Pua didn't want to take any chances on missing the birth of her first grandchild.

"*Aloha* from the beach," she answered cheerily, alerted by the Caller ID that it was Uilani's husband David.

"Auntie Pua, this is David," he announced. There was a certain politeness and formality about David that Auntie Pua liked. Uilani was reserved too, not at all like her younger sisters. She and David were well suited to each other. "This is it, Uilani's going into labor. We're ready to go out the door and head to the hospital. She's fine, *no worries*."

That's all Auntie Pua had to hear. *No worries*? Ui's going to have a baby! Putting her weight on her arms the grandmother-to-be hoisted herself out of her beach chair and walked knee deep into the water, still holding the cell phone in her hand as her eyes searched the vista once again.

Where could they be? They should be hungry by now.

She paced back and forth at the water's edge, splashing as she went, soaking the colorful *pareo* she wore over her bathing suit.

What to do, what to do?

Auntie Pua turned on her heel and headed for the path through the forest to the shady spot where they had parked the truck. Climbing into the pickup bed, she opened the large aluminum toolbox where her long-unused snorkel gear resided. With her yellow mesh dive bag in hand, Auntie Pua jumped from the truck with surprising agility and retraced her steps back to the beach.

Snugly outfitted with her gear, Auntie Pua glided along the surface, facedown in the water. She headed for the outcropping of lava rock that marked the presence of the reef, hoping to find Kalani and the kids.

Auntie Pua neared the reef and looked around at the floating bodies that were snorkeling near the anchored sailboat. None of the bathing suits belonged to Kalani or the kids. When she got close enough to read the name *Hana Hou* painted on the vessel's side, she realized they must be on the boat.

"*Aloha*, permission to come aboard," she called out in a sunny voice, concealing how she felt inside. Auntie Pua hadn't been on a boat in years.

Leilani was the first to hear her auntie and hurried over to the rope ladder to give her a hand. "Auntie, Auntie, what are you doing here?"

Twelve

Captain Kenny took a deep breath before opening the door. On the walk from the harbor to Clara Witherspoon's office he had been rehearsing how he was going to break the news about finding Johann's scarf. He was not only concerned about upsetting Mrs. Witherspoon. Captain Kenny was worried too.

He knew Johann would never abandon his scarf like that. If he no longer wanted to keep it he'd donate it to a charity fundraiser where it would be snapped-up for big bucks. Besides, Johann felt strongly about discarding things into the ocean. That was his home, not a dumping ground.

Clara Witherspoon was right after all, thought Captain Kenny. *Something's wrong.*

Mrs. Witherspoon was surprised to see Captain Kenny walk through the door. He had only visited her office once before and that was when they were forming the committee for the Johann festivities. "To what do I owe this pleasant surprise?" asked Mrs. Witherspoon, motioning toward an antique *koa* chair.

The captain sat slowly.

Mrs. Witherspoon could not hide her impatience and asked point blank, "What brings you here? It's Johann, isn't it?"

Captain Kenny took another deep breath before he began telling Mrs. Witherspoon what had happened. He had custody of Johann's precious scarf because Kalani, Pua and the kids had to swim back to shore and make tracks for the hospital to await the birth of Uilani's baby. Besides, it was easier to transport the giant scarf on the *Hana Hou* than to swim with it.

"Please, let me see it," said Mrs. Witherspoon, politely, almost reverently. Captain Kenny handed over the treasure, neatly folded in a large blue and gold shopping bag.

Mrs. Witherspoon carefully removed the scarf and partially unfolded it on her large desktop. "Yes, this is Johann's. No question about it."

She gently stroked the fine cloth with her fingertips while she pondered what to do. Captain Kenny, though usually accustomed to being the one in charge, waited patiently for Mrs. Witherspoon to speak. "At least there's no more doubt. Something is amiss," she said. "Captain, please set up a meeting with Kalani, Pua and the twins right away!"

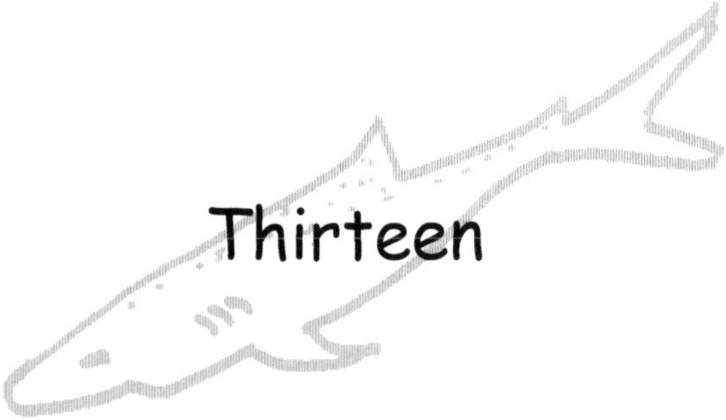

Thirteen

Mrs. Witherspoon's request that the group assemble immediately was an unrealistic expectation. Uncle Kalani had his job as a Hawaiian Studies instructor at the local college. The twins had to go to school. Captain Kenny's boating business required his attention. And Auntie Pua felt her place was with Uilani and her new baby boy. The earliest a meeting could be set up was for 4:00 p.m. the following day.

"Is that bell ever going to ring?" the normally patient Leilani whispered to Keoni who was in the row next to her. "It's taking forever."

"No kidding. The clock's in super slo-mo. C'mon, bell, ring . . . ring!"

At last the clanging of the bell signaled freedom and the twins joined their classmates in the stampede toward the door. As they left the school grounds, they saw Uncle Kalani's truck waiting at the curb, idling like a racehorse at the starting gate.

As luck would have it, traffic was flowing smoothly on the often overburdened two-lane road that ran along the *pali* or cliff side. The twins relaxed and enjoyed the view.

Surfers and sailboats floated like buoys on the sunlit sea, while cotton candy clouds in animal shapes hovered over the island of Lanai. "Hey, that cloud looks like a crocodile," said Leilani.

Arriving at their destination, the trio recognized Captain Kenny as he disappeared into the oceanfront café housed in a low-slung plantation-era building. Painted in turquoise and yellow and topped with a red tin roof, the café had outdoor tables along the seawall within a few feet of the breaking waves.

Mrs. Witherspoon had been the first to arrive, looking official as she sat at the end of a picnic table with a yellow legal pad before her. She wasted no time in getting down to business.

"Kids, we are indebted to you for finding Johann's scarf. We had our suspicions before but the scarf confirms it. It's our first and most important clue. Johann is missing!"

She cleared her throat. "Root beer floats all around," she commanded the waiter.

"Please, tell no one what's happened," she whispered. "The media could get wind of it. I'd like to keep this under our hats as long as possible. Hopefully it will be resolved quickly with no one the wiser. I've outlined a plan of action and have assignments for each of you . . . "

"Clara, hold on there," interrupted Captain Kenny. "You haven't even given anyone a chance to express how they feel about being involved. Kalani's got his work at the college and the children have school. Isn't this is a job for the authorities? They have resources—manpower, ships . . . "

"No, no, we mustn't call the authorities yet. We'd have all sorts of people mucking up the works. Let's investigate first. Please, go along with me on this."

Captain Kenny looked at the twins. The twins looked at each other and turned to their uncle, ready to follow his lead.

"What do you have in mind?" he said.

Fourteen

"Ah, Mr. Humpbach, I trust you slept well," said the voice that seemed to surround Johann. After a pause, he heard it again, big and hollow. "You are to be my guest, Mr. Humpbach!" With that, darkness exploded against the light, and Johann found himself in a sunny lagoon surrounded by a garden of iridescent coral.

The water warmed and Johann breached. He thrust himself almost completely out of the water, arched like a diver, his flippers extended. He landed on his side in a thunderous shower of spray and saw the Hawaiian sun.

"I'm glad you're back to your old self, Mr. Humpbach. I was concerned about you for a few days."

Johann recognized the tone of voice was insincere and thought, *two-faced phony*!

He realized there was nothing he could do but let events unfold. He felt his strength returning although he was sorely troubled by his predicament.

Was it true? Had he really been unconscious for days? What had happened? Wait a minute—*guest*?

The voice seemed to read Johann's mind. "Yes, you have

been out cold for days. And yes, indeed, you are my guest. You had an unfavorable reaction to a little something in the water. We do apologize for any inconvenience."

A little something in the water! *Inconvenience*! Johann thought, as he swam in a large circle. "Enough of this nonsense, I'm outa here!" he fumed, and headed out to sea.

Johann hadn't gotten very far before he realized the lagoon, except for a stretch of rocky shoreline, was surrounded on all sides by a great lava wall. It was like he was in a giant pond on the edge of the ocean. There was an entrance facing the high seas—a small opening between pillars of the stony black lava the Hawaiians called *aa*. This was fine for little creatures but something as large as a forty-ton whale could never fit through it. Johann could hear, smell and see the open ocean and freedom, but there was no way in and no way out.

He was alarmed and awed at the same time. How did they get him in here anyway?

Fifteen

Mrs. Witherspoon was about to respond to Uncle Kalani's question when the waiter arrived with tall frosty mugs containing root beer floats. Keoni and Leilani sucked up every last drop, making slurping sounds with their straws. "This hits the spot," said Keoni.

Mrs. Witherspoon began to speak. "As I said before, I have jobs for each of you. Captain Kenny, you have a lot of friends in the boating business. Can you put out feelers to see if anyone's noticed anything unusual? You must use the utmost discretion. Please try to make your inquiries without letting anyone know what's going on."

She continued, not giving the captain a chance to respond. "I, myself, am in touch with Native American leaders from the Northwest whom I met when they came to the islands for the Festival of Canoes." They all knew that she had been responsible for coordinating this successful event. Carvers from all around the Pacific Rim had come to build their canoes in the traditional way, made from a single log. "My contacts can check around Johann's home port so we can determine exactly when he left Alaskan waters."

The twins sat attentively, waiting for their turn as Mrs. Witherspoon flipped through the pages of her yellow legal pad. "Kalani, you are well known and respected by the *kupuna* of this island. What would be the chances of your asking them to consult with their *aumakua*? Perhaps these guardian spirits may be aware of something that could help us."

Kalani thought for a moment, rubbing his chin, and nodded his okay.

Mrs. Witherspoon made notations as the others sat silently. She smiled warmly, and looked back and forth between the twins. "Keoni and Leilani, once again I can't thank you enough for finding Johann's scarf. I appreciate your not telling any of your friends about it. I know it's a big secret and if I were in your slippers, I'd have a hard time keeping my mouth shut. Would you be willing to return to the cave where you found the scarf? Maybe there are other clues down there that could give us a lead."

The twins made no attempt to conceal their excitement at the thought of a sailing and diving expedition. They grinned from ear to ear, forming deep dimples at the corners of their mouths. Their eyes widened and they nodded their heads in approval.

That settled, Mrs. Witherspoon turned her attention back to the captain. "Captain Kenny, I'd like you to take the twins back to the area of the cave. It would be better than snorkeling out from shore just in case they find something. It will give them a place to rest between dives too. Of course, Kalani, you'd accompany the kids. I think we all agree it's not a good idea for them to dive alone. I've heard what great swimmers they are," she continued, "but we must err on the side of caution."

All eyes were on Captain Kenny. It was his turn to speak. "It's a sound plan, I guess. But this is a small island, and sooner or later word of our inquiries is bound to get out. You know how relentless the 'coconut wireless' is. Noe already knows about this and promised not to say anything, but she could let something slip. I'll do my best, but I'm not sure I can ask around without arousing suspicions."

"I have complete confidence in you, Captain," said Mrs. Witherspoon, as she raised her eyebrows and looked over the rim of her glasses. She turned to Uncle Kalani. "Kalani?"

"I'll talk to the *kupuna*. But if we want their help, their *kokua*, I'll have to tell them what's really going on. I think we can count on their silence, for a while anyway. And, I'm willing to go along on the dive. There is one other thing though. Has anyone thought about what Pua is going to say?"

Keoni and Leilani instantly knew what Uncle Kalani was talking about. Auntie Pua was strict about the twins' schoolwork. There was also the matter of their perfect attendance record and the award it would bring at the end of the school year.

And then there was that thing she had about boats. The twins were floored when they got the tickets to the Whale Song Tour. It had taken some convincing on Uncle Kalani's part to get her to go along with the idea. And knowing Auntie Pua, if she thought something bad had happened to Johann, she might think the whole thing was just too dangerous.

Sixteen

She had only been home a few minutes when Auntie Pua heard Uncle Kalani's truck in the driveway. She had been with Uilani and the baby since early that morning and stayed until David came home from work.

Auntie Pua was as tired as a sugar mill worker on Friday. All she wanted to do was seize the sofa and have an icy ginger ale. Maybe she would allow herself the luxury of watching the food channel after dinner.

But there was something strange about the way Uncle Kalani and the kids acted when they came home. Auntie Pua picked up on it right away.

"You guys all look like the cat that swallowed the canary. What's up?"

"How was your day, Pua? How's everyone doing? Tell us all about it," said Uncle Kalani, trying to change the subject.

"Sorry," said Auntie Pua sounding grumpy, "but I don't feel like discussing my day right now. Everyone's fine, no worries."

Auntie Pua was clearly not in the mood to be trifled with.

Taking the hint, Uncle Kalani went to the kitchen to get

himself something to drink. The twins went to their rooms. After dropping off their backpacks they bumped into each other in the middle of the hall.

"Shhh, come into my room and close the door," whispered Leilani.

"Auntie Pua knows something's up. She's just too tired to deal with it now. She's gotta let us go! Everyone's counting on us, Keoni. We know where to look. *Shoots*, it'd be so much fun, sailing on the *Hana Hou* and diving again."

There was not much talk during dinner since everyone was famished. The stir-fried chicken with vegetables and rice was simple but tasty. Auntie Pua had the taste buds to be a fine chef if she'd wanted to. She could make a delicious meal out of just about anything.

Uncle Kalani was a slow eater and was taking the last bite with his chopsticks when Auntie Pua popped the question. "So, how was your meeting with Clara Witherspoon? I bet she made a big deal about you finding the scarf. I'm sure Johann's gonna be pleased when it's returned to him and he hears how you rescued it. I bet he'll want to meet you."

There was no getting around it. Someone had to speak up. "Auntie, Johann's missing and we've been asked to help find him," said Leilani.

"Johann's missing? And what do you mean, help?" asked Auntie Pua.

"He should have been here by now," said Uncle Kalani. He explained the significance of finding the scarf and why Mrs. Witherspoon wanted the kids to look for more clues at the lava cave. "I'd be there with them. Captain Kenny was drafted into taking us out on his boat. We'd like to go tomorrow morning."

"I see," said Auntie Pua, looking about as pleased as a grounded teenager on Friday night. "What about school? What about your perfect attendance? What about your award?"

"Well, Auntie, that's the point. We haven't missed any school so one day isn't a big deal and we don't have any tests tomorrow. And the award—it's just a piece of paper."

"Wouldn't you get to go to a movie too . . . and a trip to the bowling alley?"

"Please, please," begged Keoni, "we'd rather go sailing and diving."

"Mrs. Witherspoon really needs our help. We know where to look," said Leilani.

"What about you, Kalani? What about work?"

"I don't have any morning classes tomorrow. We'd take off about 6:30 and be back by 11:00. The best visibility is in the morning. That's when the water's nice and calm."

It had started out calm that day too, thought Auntie Pua, picturing her younger sister Malia. She remembered how joyful they had been when the twins were born and Malia asked Auntie Pua to be their Godmother. Such happy times.

And then, *auwe*, the tragedy. Malia and her husband Kimo had gone fishing on their day off, just the two of them. They had been married seven years and were very much in love. The twins were six at the time and spending the day with Auntie Pua and Uncle Kalani.

There had been no small craft warnings that morning but suddenly the weather turned ugly. The Kona storm struck with the ferocity of a fire-breathing dragon. A distress signal had been sent from the *Malia I,* Kimo's boat, but the twins' parents were never found. Wreckage from the boat turned up but Kimo and Malia were lost to the sea forever.

It had fallen upon Auntie Pua to comfort her niece and nephew. She had spoken to them gently. "Your mommy and daddy are at home in the sea. That's where their ancestors came from. They will welcome them. And they'll be together until the end of time. That's the most important thing."

Keoni held Leilani's tiny hand as they bravely received the news. The memory almost brought Auntie Pua to tears.

The sound of Uncle Kalani clearing his throat brought her back to the present. "What if something bad happened to Johann? There isn't any danger, is there?"

"Oh, no, Auntie. It's just a simple morning dive," said Leilani. "We can even go to our classes after lunch."

Seventeen

Captain Kenny tried to appear casual.

"*Howzit*? Seen any whales yet?"

"They seem late this year."

Naturally the subject of Johann came up. Wasn't he overdue? Had he been heard from? The investigation was stimulating concern about Johann's whereabouts, the opposite of what Mrs. Witherspoon had intended.

Captain Kenny was growing tired of evading questions and not getting any answers. He was about to give up when he ran into an old friend, the captain of a cruise ship that plied Hawaiian waters.

"What's that? You haven't seen any whales yet? Heck, we have. Saw one a few days ago between Maui and the Big Island. Put on a darn good show too, popping up all over the place. Passengers loved it! Gee, thought I heard'm singing!"

"Johann! You saw Johann? What day did you see him exactly? Did you see him swim off? Which way did he go? Toward Maui waters you say?"

Captain Kenny tried to conceal his excitement and

tactfully disengage himself from the conversation with the cruise ship captain. But his old friend was in a talkative mood and it wasn't easy to break away. By the time Captain Kenny was free it was well after 9 p.m. before he could call Mrs. Witherspoon with the news.

"*Mahalo* for calling, Captain. This is valuable information. Now we know for certain Johann is in Hawaiian waters. Let's see what tomorrow brings."

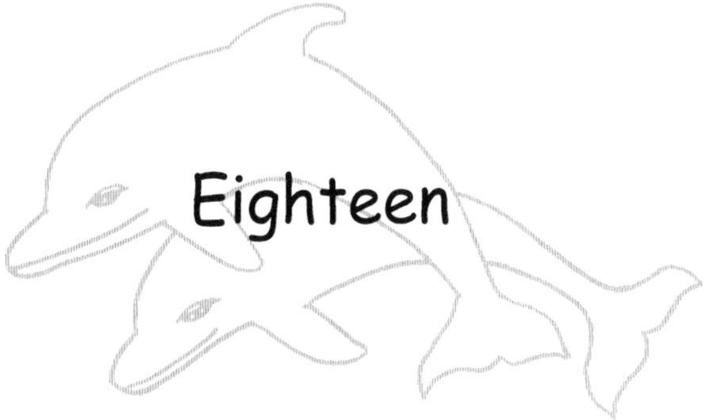

Eighteen

The twins awoke to the aroma of sticky buns baking in the oven, luring them from their cozy beds even though it was still dark. The sound of running water and the banging of the iron skillet Auntie Pua used to make Spam and eggs announced the house was coming to life. They could hear the familiar slam of the creaky wooden screen door as Uncle Kalani ferried their gear and a cooler of food and beverages out to the truck.

Keoni and Leilani wore zippered sweatshirts over their rash guards and bathing suits to protect them from the predawn chill. They brought their binoculars along to search for signs of whales.

"You guys have fun out there but don't do anything foolish," said Auntie Pua. She gave them each a hug then waved them off with a *shaka*, the Hawaiian gesture for *hang loose*. Auntie Pua stood in the driveway until Kalani's truck was out of sight. Adjusting her kimono around her a little more tightly, she retied the sash and headed into the house to go about her morning chores before heading off to Ui and David's.

Smiling at the prospect of their expedition, the trio looked forward to searching for clues to Johann's whereabouts. As they headed across the island to the harbor where the *Hana Hou* was berthed, the sun came up turning the clouds an electric coral-pink. With little traffic at this hour they arrived at the harbor well ahead of time. Captain Kenny was already on the dock, chatting with Charlie as he gathered his long blond hair into a ponytail.

By 6:45 a.m. the *Hana Hou* had cleared the harbor and set sail for the southeastern part of the island and the ancient lava flow that marked the area of the underwater cave.

The air was fresh and clean and the water sparkled like Tiffany diamonds. Keoni and Leilani sat comfortably on the deck, their legs stretched out before them as if they were seated in deck chairs on a luxury liner. They watched the land fall away as they sailed from shore. A recent rain had greened the mountainsides that had been brown too long. Buildings and boats that lined the shore began to look like toys.

The twins took turns with their binoculars, scanning the water for signs of whales. They were treated to a visit from a family of bottlenose dolphins, the kind that seemed to wear a smile. They counted five in the dolphin party swimming alongside the *Hana Hou*. But there were no whales. No Johann.

"This is great!" shouted Leilani, her face welcoming the ocean spray as the *Hana Hou* cut through the water like a surfboard through a south swell. The sailboat listed to one side and the twins gripped the wooden rail, hanging on tight.

"This is better than 'the Ring of Fire' at the county fair!" bellowed Keoni, the thrill in his voice nearly lost in the wind.

"For real!" yelled Leilani, her heart pounding. "Awesome!"

When the vessel had righted itself, the captain called out, "Who wants to steer?" Keoni and Leilani both jumped at the chance to take a turn at the wheel. Charlie kept an eye on them. Though only in his twenties, he was an experienced sailor and a natural teacher too.

The vessel slowed as they neared their destination with Keoni at the wheel. Captain Kenny and Charlie expertly moored the boat, dropping anchor in the sandy bottom below.

Uncle Kalani and the twins got into their gear and jumped off the deck into water as clear as the Ocean Center aquarium. They swam toward the finger of lava that pointed to the cave below. Would it give up another secret?

Almost immediately Leilani spied something odd sticking out of the sand. She propelled herself to the cave's open mouth and tried to free the object from the grasp of the sea floor. Keoni swam to her side to help.

Without warning, the calm sea started to churn. The mild current turned strong and the water became murky as it mixed with the whirling sand. Almost as abruptly as it had begun the maelstrom stopped. Uncle Kalani stared at the spot where the twins had been just seconds before.

Where were they? He spun in a circle, looking up and looking down. There was no sign of Keoni or Leilani. He was running out of breath and had no choice but to head for the surface. They must have gone up without him.

Nineteen

JOHANN MISSING! TWINS LOST IN SEARCH FOR CLUES! Headlines around the world proclaimed the news.

When Uncle Kalani surfaced he found that the twins were not safely on board the *Hana Hou* and that Captain Kenny had also experienced the sudden tumult. As Charlie told it, "The boat rolled so violently the captain bounced off the rail and landed on the deck like a sacked quarterback. *Shoots*, broke his arm."

Captain Kenny's pain was minor compared to Uncle Kalani's. Although he had been as diligent as a secret service agent guarding the president, he held himself responsible for the twins' disappearance. No amount of reasoning could convince him otherwise.

Even though Captain Kenny immediately called the Coast Guard for assistance Uncle Kalani dove and dove again to the point of exhaustion, hoping, praying for a glimpse of yellow or blue. Within the hour a Coast Guard helicopter appeared carrying four Navy SEALS who parachuted into the Pacific in a joint rescue effort. At nightfall they continued their search with dive lights and floodlights from the

Coast Guard vessel that had joined them.

A second Coast Guard ship followed the current out to sea, another scoured the beaches and rocky coastline. The resolute divers covered every inch of the now famous cave that a millennia ago had been a tube housing a river of flowing lava. They came upon a dead-end, a wall of smooth, water-washed rock leading nowhere.

By the next morning nearly every available boat joined in the hunt too, but as the search grew bigger, hope grew dimmer.

All that Mrs. Witherspoon had hoped to avoid with her careful and discreet planning had disastrously come to pass. The story of Johann and the twins' disappearance ignited a maelstrom on land that rivaled the one under the sea. Even Charlie had to turn off his phone to get a moment's peace.

TV news teams swept the island competing for angles. Anyone who dared to step outside risked being accosted. Reporters went to the school, they went to the harbor and they patrolled the towns searching for stories.

Clara Witherspoon replayed the events leading up to the tragedy over and over in her mind. *What could I have been thinking? If it weren't for me the twins would be alive and well.* Mr. Witherspoon tried his best, but there was no consoling her.

Captain Kenny, despite his calm exterior, was churning inside. *If I hadn't gone along with Clara Witherspoon's scheme none of this would have happened,* thought the captain. *Why did I do it anyway? The children are gone and for what, a few more ticket and T-shirt sales?*

Fortunately, Auntie Pua had the comfort of family around her when she got the call from Uncle Kalani. She was about to collapse when David and Uilani caught her. They maintained their composure as best they could. "We must be strong for Auntie Pua," they said.

When darkness fell Captain Kenny headed the *Hana Hou* back toward the harbor and docked the boat one step ahead of the first wave of reporters to descend upon the island.

It was a postcard perfect night. A full moon loomed large over the silhouetted mountain Haleakala and lights from hotels strung along the shore twinkled as if it were Christmas. Understandably, Uncle Kalani did not appreciate the splendor. On the drive home he had to stop by the side of the road more than once to pull himself together.

Uncle Kalani, the pillar of strength, felt a sadness he didn't know existed. "Pua. I need Pua," he cried to himself, clutching the steering wheel. And Pua needed him.

Twenty

There was no area of the lagoon Johann hadn't explored. He swam over, around and through the exquisite coral but was not interested in its beauty. He was looking for a way out. He could hear the waves breaking outside the rocky wall. Finding a way to reach them was another story.

The silence was eerie and Johann didn't like it. He didn't feel like singing either, which was unusual. Besides, he didn't want to invite the attention of his captor.

Hmm, what's that? he thought. Something odd was on a rocky shelf nearby. It's light was faint at first but it grew brighter, a blue dot glowing like a speck of neon. Upon closer inspection he spied a tiny, sorrowful looking squid. The little creature froze with fright when he saw the gigantic whale.

Johann remembered hearing something about reef squid glowing a brilliant blue when stressed or startled. He sought to reassure the little creature. "Now, now, no one's going to hurt you. Besides, I already ate. Ha, ha."

The tentacled mollusk looked warily at the gentle giant. As the jest sank in, he slowly relaxed, his blueness fading.

Johann introduced himself. "I'm Johann Sebastian

Humpbach, tenor and pilot whale, of the humpbacks of Hawaii and Alaska. Who are you?"

Johann's voice was huge even though he tried to speak softly. The little squid tumbled in the wake created by the great whale's words. But he righted himself and in a thin, squeaky voice blurted out, "I'm Sonny Squid and I've lost my family!" Sensing he had a sympathetic ear, Sonny started to turn blue once again.

Johann's first instinct was to try to cheer up Sonny with a song.

Cheer up, little guy,
it can't be that bad
What is it that makes you
feel so sad?

Sonny appreciated the sympathy but was aggravated too. "Don't you listen? I told you, I lost my family!"

"Sonny, please tell me what happened," said Johann.

"It was that . . . that mean, bad man, Dr. Vile. That's what they called him. He and his friends . . . they took away my mom and dad and all my brothers and sisters. I'm the littlest so I slipped through the net. I heard him say he was going to squeeze every last drop out of them. Their ink, he took them for their ink!"

Sonny started to shiver. "He was going to mix it with something. He said he was going to 'flood the sea and bring that big whale to me.' Those were his exact words. I heard him. Then they carried off my mom and dad and, and . . . "

Poor Sonny. He started glowing all over again.

Twenty-one

Mrs. Witherspoon's office was under siege. When she entered the museum she saw a gaggle of reporters waiting by her door. Unseen, she made an about-face, pulled her straw hat lower on her head and put her sunglasses back on. Retracing her steps she hurried outside.

Where to now, old girl?

Almost without thinking Clara Witherspoon headed toward Captain Kenny's office down by the harbor. *I wonder if he's there*, she thought.

As she neared the enclave she could make out the *Hana Hou's* mast and identifying flags in the distance. The sailboat slumbered at its berth.

Mrs. Witherspoon cautiously approached the old building that housed the captain's office. The coast was clear. She made a dash for the entrance, yanked hard on the weathered door, and sprinted up the narrow staircase to the second floor landing. Faded letters stenciled on the door at the top of the stairs read: Hana Hou, Suite 202.

Noe greeted Mrs. Witherspoon's sudden appearance in her usual lilting voice, "Clara Witherspoon, how you doing?

We were worried about you."

"About me? What about those poor kids? And Pua and Kalani? Me? I'm the last one anyone should be worried about," she said before catching her lapse in manners. "Ah, *mahalo* for your concern, Noe. Is the captain in?"

"He sneaked out for a sandwich but he should be back any minute. He's incognito, too."

No sooner had Noe spoken than there were footsteps on the creaky wooden stairs. The door flew open and was quickly shut—the entrance of a fugitive.

Captain Kenny had his paper bag lunch in one hand, his other arm in a cast. He was nearly unrecognizable in a large straw hat and dark glasses.

"Ah, Clara. I was going to call you."

Any blame Captain Kenny or Mrs. Witherspoon may have placed on the other had evaporated. Now they were united in guilt, self-doubt and loss.

"I feel so helpless," confessed Mrs. Witherspoon. "We've got to find those children."

"I feel the same way. Maybe it's wishful thinking but I think there's a chance they're still alive. After all, no bodies have been found . . . "

"Yes, you're right. They're alive! I just know it. Let's call Pua and Kalani and tell them how we feel!"

Hold on, Captain Kenny told himself. *You're being swept away by the Clara tide again.* "Now, Clara, shouldn't we think this through before we give them false hope? There's no evidence . . . "

"No, no, let's call them now."

Auntie Pua and Uncle Kalani were holed up at Uilani and David's to avoid the reporters who had staked out their house. When they hadn't answered their phone the captain called Uilani's, not knowing if Pua and Kalani would be there or want to speak with him if they were.

As luck would have it Auntie Pua answered Ui's phone. Captain Kenny asked if they could meet. Mrs. Witherspoon and Captain Kenny would come to them. Yes, within the hour.

Mrs. Witherspoon and Captain Kenny didn't know what kind of reception to expect as they approached the little *up-country* cottage. Like most island homes a jumble of shoes and rubber slippers marked the entrance to the house. Auntie Pua answered the door on the first knock. Giving Mrs. Witherspoon and Captain Kenny silent hugs she ushered them into Ui's sunny kitchen.

Auntie Pua was a forgiving sort and in her sorrow knew the others were grieving too. No guilt, no blame . . . that was Auntie Pua. Uncle Kalani quietly hung in the background, waiting to hear what their visitors had to say.

"We think the twins are alive and perhaps their disappearance is connected to Johann's," said Mrs. Witherspoon.

"Bear in mind, we don't have anything to support this," said Captain Kenny, "it may be wishful thinking, but I don't think we should give up hope just yet."

Much to everyone's surprise, Auntie Pua nodded in agreement. She spoke firmly. "It's not like when Malia and Kimo were lost. I knew then they were gone for good. I can't explain it, but I have a strong feeling . . . somewhere, somehow, Leilani and Keoni are still among the living."

Twenty-two

The warm sun beat down on Leilani's back as she lay sprawled in the surf on a bed of polished stones. She slowly lifted her head and looked around, then lowered it back to the ground to ease the dizziness that came over her.

The glistening stones made a tinkling sound as they clinked together when the tide washed over them. It was soothing.

"Lei . . . Leilani, are you okay?" said Keoni, a quiet urgency in his voice. He shook his sister gently by the shoulder as he squatted beside her.

"Ow, my head hurts," she moaned, rolling onto her side.

"Let me have a look at that," said Keoni, concerned about the big scrape on Leilani's forehead. It was bruised and swollen. Her knees and the palms of her hands were scuffed up too.

"Keoni, where are we? What happened?" said Leilani managing to sit up and check her hands and knees for damage.

"It was like this tornado came out of nowhere and everything started swirling. My mask got ripped off and I had to close my eyes real tight because there was so much sand in the water. I tumbled over and over but I relaxed like you should do when you get caught in a shore break. It felt like I was being sucked through some kind of goop."

"Wow. All I remember is getting spun around and feeling like I was being sandblasted! Where's Uncle Kalani? He must be here too."

Keoni helped Leilani rise to her feet as she dusted off the small pebbles that clung to her wet skin. Their fins, masks and snorkels were gone. With an eye out for Uncle Kalani and their precious gear they checked out their surroundings.

It looked like they had washed up on the beach of a large turquoise lagoon. It was encircled by a giant lava wall. They recognized that the rocky sides were probably formed hundreds of years ago by lava flowing down the mountain into the sea. But the part of the wall that faced the horizon looked like it was man made, and was not the work of Pele, goddess of the volcano.

Shiny rocks made smooth by the sea littered the coarse, black sand. The beach was a narrow horseshoe of a place, sealed off on the *mauka* side by a dense bougainvillea hedge of blazing color. While pleasing to the eye, they knew bougainvillea was a dangerous beauty. Its thorns could lacerate the unwary with its spiky whip-like branches.

"There's no way we can go over or through this hedge," said Keoni. "It looks like we're stuck here."

The twins picked their way along the shoreline in both directions but there was no flotsam, no snorkels, no fins to be found. Most importantly, there was no Uncle Kalani. They were on their own.

"Now what?" asked Leilani. She felt confused, and her head was throbbing.

"Hey, look over there!" said Keoni, pointing to what looked like an opening in the black wall. "*Shoots*, I wish we had our binoculars now. From here it looks like it's big enough for us to swim through."

"Swim out in the open ocean? With no fins? I dunno, Keoni . . . "

Leilani's protest was interrupted by the unmistakable sound of a whale spouting—*whoosh*. Now alert, her eyes were fixed in the direction of the sound. "Did you see that!" she exclaimed as a waterspout erupted from the water's surface not a hundred yards away. Less than a minute later a big humpback appeared, rising with grace and seemingly without effort from below. The huge whale glided through the water and arched his back exposing recognizable and distinctive white flukes.

"It's Johann! It's Johann!" The twins screamed with delight, jumping up and down, forgetting their plight.

Like a clap of thunder out of nowhere Leilani was seized mid-air by a pair of rough hands. The assailant carried her under his tattooed arm with ease though Leilani did not go lightly. Struggling and kicking with all her might she screamed, "Help! Help!" at the top of her lungs.

Keoni was grabbed too and though a big hand covered his eyes he could see through the spaces between callused fingers. He thought he saw the hedge move, creating an opening just big enough for a large man and a struggling twin to go through.

Twenty-three

Sonny Squid was glowing more intensely now, pulsating like a runner's heart after a marathon. "What can I do to help you, Sonny?" asked Johann. Out of the blue he and Sonny found themselves surrounded by all manner of creatures. They had emerged from their hiding places in the deep recesses of the coral all at once, like a cloud of butterflies. They came to comfort Sonny but out of curiosity, too. So this was the famous Johann Sebastian Humpbach.

Bits and pieces of information bombarded Johann. The whole population of the reef came to him with their stories: Moorish idols, handsomely striped in yellow and black. The state fish *humuhumunukunukuapua'a* with their bandit eyes. Parrot fish in rainbow hues and butterfly fish with needle noses. Leilani's favorite, the comical trumpet fish, darted about. Even the reclusive eels and octopuses came out of hiding. Reef sharks visited too, the small, white-tipped kind. The little reef fish, usually scared to death of the sharks, seemed to feel safe with Johann there.

All this prattle was quite startling, especially since a short time ago it had been so quiet. The cacophony began to recede as the creatures got their grievances off their chests.

As it calmed down Johann thought he heard children's voices excitedly call out his name.

What he heard puzzled him. What he thought were joyful sounds had turned into cries for help and then . . . silence.

"What was that?" Johann, asked his newly found friends. The community of creatures that hung on Johann's every word thought they heard it too.

A crackle-voiced seabird told a trumpet fish, who told Sonny, who told Johann that he saw a couple of men carry off two children through the bushes.

Could this incident be related to this Dr. Vile that his fellow creatures had told him about? It was not only Sonny who had a sad story to tell. They all had terrible experiences of one kind or another.

Johann heard that men had tried to capture reef fish using electroshocks in the water. They were after the colorful creatures to sell to pet shops on the mainland. They blasted away bits of coral with dynamite to flush out their prey and hacked at the reef with hammers, their ill-gotten chunks of coral fetching a hefty price. And, what Johann thought was the lowest thing of all, they dumped unwanted and damaged fish back into the water only to have them wash ashore and rot in the hot sun.

This was heavy stuff thought Johann. He was the *guest* of a wicked man who, besides killing and torturing fish and destroying the reef, had kidnapped two children. He'd captured Johann too, apparently by spreading some kind of drug mixed with squid ink in the water.

But why? Why would anyone go to all that trouble? What on earth did this Dr. Vile want with him?

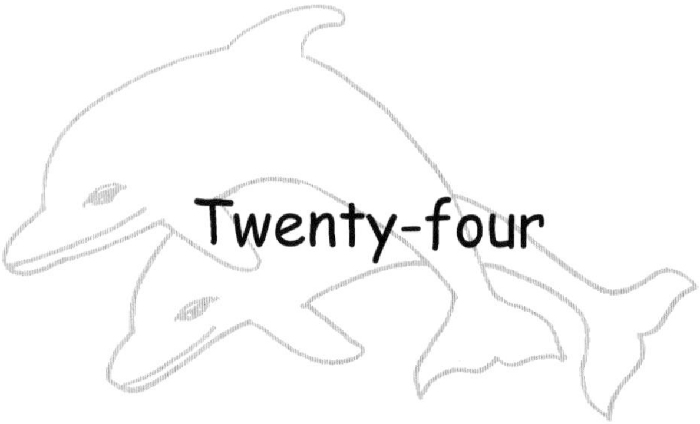

Twenty-four

The meeting with the *kupuna* had gone well. "We will do everything in our power to connect with our *aumakua* and help to find the missing *keiki*," they pledged to Uncle Kalani.

There was nothing else the foursome who'd met in Uilani's kitchen could think to do. The search by the Coast Guard was winding down and nothing more had been found. They had Johann's scarf and that was it. Not a lot to go on.

The only logical next step was to have Uncle Kalani ask for help from the *kupuna*. This had been part of the plan to find Johann all along but had been put off because of the twins' disappearance.

The next day word came from Uncle Oliver. "I dreamed the twins were floating in a turquoise sky surrounded by clouds of lava," he said.

Turquoise sky? Clouds of lava? What did that mean?

There was something else. The *kupuna* described a large whale that seemed trapped, unsuccessful in his attempt to swim through the lava clouds.

What was the dream's significance? They thought and

thought. It was Uncle Kalani who came up with the idea of the ancient Hawaiian fishpond. He'd lived on the island all his life and knew of places like that.

"In olden days the Hawaiians would build ponds on the edge of the sea and deposit their catch there so they would have plenty of food even if they were unable to fish," Uncle Kalani explained. "There was a small opening in the rocks so the water could circulate and be refreshed by the ocean. Often small fish would swim in and then grow too large to swim out. It was an ingenious system and served the ancient Hawaiians well."

With little else to go on, the gang of four decided to begin a search for a large fishpond, mindful that Uncle Oliver's vision was just a dream.

"It isn't much but at least it's something," admitted Uncle Kalani, his spirits buoyed. They all felt better because at least now they had a sense of purpose.

"We promise to hold a picture of Keoni and Leilani in our minds, a vision of them alive and well," they vowed to one another.

Twenty-five

Leilani was roused from her slumber by the sound of a key turning in the lock. Her heart pounded as heavy feet approached the luxurious bed where she lay still, playing dead. The footsteps paused then retreated, and the door slammed shut, not giving her a chance to see who her visitor might be.

The last thing she remembered was a soggy cloth with a sickening odor pressing upon her face. Though she was slowly coming to her senses, things were still fuzzy. She couldn't believe her eyes when she saw a glass of milk, a hamburger and fries on the bedside table.

Leilani gobbled down the burger and fries like a contestant in a hot dog eating contest. Annie Pua would have scolded her for inhaling her food like that and Keoni would have teased her for pigging out.

Only after she had devoured every crumb did Leilani become aware of the throbbing in her head. She felt like someone was tapping her skull softly with a hammer. Her scrapes and bruises were painful to the touch though a gauze bandage patched her forehead and her knees were dressed with a soothing ointment.

Leilani sank into a cocoon of soft pillows and surveyed her surroundings for the first time. The room looked like something out of the magazines in the beauty shop where Auntie Pua had her hair done. The paintings on the walls were framed in gold, their giant flowers staring back at her. The windows and ceilings were twice as high as the ones at Leilani's house. Although a pair of tall, slender lamps with silken shades radiated a warm and pleasing glow, the room didn't seem right for a tropical island. It was a room that belonged in a faraway place. "More money than sense," Auntie Pua would say.

Suddenly it struck her. She was alone! There was no Keoni! Where was he? Was he okay? Her heart started to race once again. She jumped from the bed and ran to the window, pulling back the brocaded drapes. It was black outside. No moon, no stars, no light.

She headed for the door and gave it a yank, knowing deep down it was probably locked. And it was. She inspected every inch of the plush bedroom and adjoining marble bath with its gold fixtures and gold monogrammed towels—DV? She searched under the bed, opened every drawer, every closet . . .

She was a prisoner in that room.

Leilani exhaled. She felt afraid, like an orphan abandoned in an unknown street. "Be cool," she had to tell herself, over and over.

Leilani tried to rest but tossed and turned. She looked around the room wishing Auntie Pua could see it. Oh, how she missed her auntie. How long had it been since they were together? Leilani didn't know how much time had passed or even what day it was.

She remembered Auntie Pua as she had last seen her, standing in the driveway in her kimono. Tears started to trickle down Leilani's face and she felt more alone than she had ever been in her young life. Keoni, Auntie Pua and Uncle Kalani had always been there for her. Where were they now?

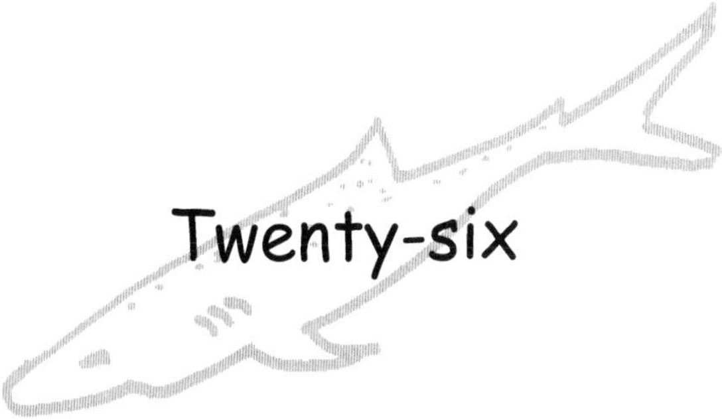

Twenty-six

It was not out of the kindness of his heart that Dr. Vile fashioned such a comfortable prison for Leilani. While the twins' kidnapping had not been premeditated, it had been necessary. "Maybe we can use it to our advantage," said Dr. Vile to his cohorts. "Play the hand you're dealt," he added, quoting one of his favorite mottoes.

The timing was not ideal as Dr. Vile was expecting other "guests." Leilani had kicked up such a fuss when they brought her in that she had to be sedated. It certainly wouldn't be acceptable to have her heard by Dr. Vile's important visitors.

Keoni on the other hand knew it would be useless to struggle. The person who hauled him off was so large and strong Keoni didn't even have wiggle room.

Dr. Vile's henchmen had carried their unexpected company through the bushes, where a brush with bougainvillea left a long scratch on Keoni's bare leg. Keoni was taken indoors and dumped into a small pantry, the door locked behind him. He tried to pick himself up off the tiled floor but began to feel dizzy. With his back to the wall, he slid to the floor once again.

Keoni felt like warmed-over toast, half-baked and crummy. He struggled to open his eyes, alerted by the sound of the door opening. A man large enough to be a sumo wrestler filled the small room with his presence. His shaved and shiny head seemed too small for his huge body and a bulbous nose dominated his face. He took Keoni by the shoulders with his bear-like hands and whispered, "You're going to be a good boy now, aren't you?"

I don't have much choice, thought Keoni.

He was taken down a darkly wallpapered hallway and escorted into a small sitting room. The hostile looking big man told him to wait quietly, closing and locking the door behind him. On the glass-topped coffee table was a tray of fast food— a hamburger, fries and a glass of milk.

Keoni was worried about his sister. Where was she? Why had they been separated? He hated not knowing if Leilani was safe but he was starving so he ate.

Keoni had just finished off the last of the fries when a smooth, slightly accented voice came from loudspeakers embedded in the ceiling. "We seem to have a problem here. You have unluckily stumbled upon Johann and I'm afraid we can't let anybody know of his whereabouts. You are to be my guest for a while. Leilani is fine and resting. It's too bad things had to turn out this way but this is what you get for nosing around where you don't belong, Keoni!"

With that the loudspeaker sputtered off and there was silence once again. "Keoni?" How did the mystery man know his name, and Leilani's too? What was going on here?

The door opened abruptly and the big man came back for Keoni, marching him down the hallway like a prison guard taking an inmate to his cell. The staircase off the kitchen was too narrow for the big man, who brushed the walls with the sides of his body as he climbed up to the second floor. He prodded Keoni in the back with his finger and it felt like a gun. They turned left at the top of the stairs and the menacing escort steered Keoni to a door at the end of the long hall.

The henchman wasted no time in unlocking the solid hardwood door and gave Keoni a little shove inside before locking up once again. The room was dimly lit with the warm glow from a pair of tall lamps.

Keoni's heart jumped. There was Leilani, her slender form barely discernable, asleep under the covers of an enormous bed.

Twenty-seven

The minute Dr. Vile's voice permeated the lagoon, the creatures of the reef vanished into their hiding places in a flurry of bubbles. Johann found himself alone, that is except for Sonny.

"It's nice to see you're making yourself at home, Mr. Humpbach," said Dr. Vile. "Now I'd like you to do me a favor."

Ah-oh. Here it comes, thought Johann, relieved and yet apprehensive to find out what this was all about.

"Mr. Humpbach, at precisely 7:00 p.m. this evening I'd like you to sing for us. Something of your choice of course. Please be prepared. We will notify you when it's time. What say you, Mr. Humpbach?"

In the loudest voice he could muster and without deliberation, Johann let out a thunderous, "No way!"

"Mr. Humpbach, may I remind you that you are my *guest* here! I am no longer asking you, I am telling you. You *will* sing at 7:00 this evening."

"In your dreams," Johann grumbled. Then he bellowed loud and clear, "The chances are slim and none and Slim just left town!" Chuckles came from the recesses of the reef.

"Very funny, Humpbach," responded the irritated Dr. Vile. "I'm afraid you have no choice in the matter. You will sing!"

"While I live to sing, I will not sing for you," Johann announced defiantly. "That's final!"

"Those are strong words, my friend, but I think I may have something that will change your mind. Let's call it an, ah, incentive. Are you familiar with two of your biggest fans—Keoni and Leilani?"

Twenty-eight

Keoni did not have the heart to wake his sleeping sister although he was dying to talk to her. He didn't want to be caught off-guard again so he stationed himself in one of the plush chairs opposite the door. He fell asleep within minutes.

His curled-up body was the first thing Leilani saw when she opened her eyes. She shook him gently. "Keoni, wake up. Please, Keoni, wake up."

Keoni moaned and rolled his head, forcing his eyes open. Leilani spoke softly but urgently into his ear. "Where are we, Keoni? I'm scared."

He put a finger to his lips and in a hushed voice told Leilani what had happened. "For sure it was Johann we saw in the lagoon. They're holding us here to keep us from telling. *The voice* guy knows our names. He also has some scary people working for him.

"What are we going to do? The door's locked, and then there's that big man I told you about. What if he comes back?"

"Let's check out the window," said Leilani, crossing the spacious room to the tall arched window. Keoni joined her.

They saw nothing but darkness, black as lava.

"Too black," observed Keoni. "And look, Lei, no stars!" Yet there were no clouds to be seen.

Keoni tried the window. "Hello! It's unlocked!" He dislodged the large, wood frame, moving it slightly. Leilani lent her strength and together they gave it a good push. It flew open!

Leilani leaned forward and her face touched—not cool nighttime air—but a black cloth that hung on the outside of the house covering the window.

Keoni pulled aside the heavy curtain and let in the morning sun.

Twenty-nine

From the second story bedroom window of Dr. Vile's house Keoni and Leilani gazed at the lagoon. The huge inlet was as calm as a bathtub full of water. Sparkling under the brilliant sun the colors changed from blues to greens and shades in between, like a fire opal under a jeweler's lamp.

There in the distance Johann was swimming, his movements fluid like a hula dancer's.

"Why would they go to all the trouble to cover the window?" whispered Leilani.

"Who knows? To make it seem like nighttime? Or maybe so no one would see Johann."

"It's so weird," said Leilani. She sighed and shrugged her shoulders. "Now what? How do we get outa here? It's a big drop. Look how far we are from the ground.

"I know what," she said, her eyes widening, "let's tie the sheets together, like in the movies."

Keoni nodded in silent agreement and they got to work.

Leilani poked a hole in the sheet using the sharp edge of a bronze leaf on one of the lamps. Tearing the large sheets into strips made a ripping sound they hoped no one could hear. The prisoners twisted and knotted the lengths of cloth to make a rope that could reach the ground.

As the rope neared completion, Leilani sounded the alarm, "Someone's coming!" Silently they gathered up their handiwork and stuffed it beneath the massive bed. Diving under an embroidered quilt, they pretended to be asleep.

The footsteps out in the hallway got closer and a key turned in the lock. The twins could sense a large presence enter the room and stand next to the bed. Their visitor may have been there only twenty seconds, but to the twins it seemed like forever. They were as still as mummies in a tomb, barely daring to breathe.

Once the coast was clear, Keoni leapt out of bed and retrieved the sheet-rope from its hiding place. "Let's finish this and *hele* on," he whispered as his nimble fingers tied the last of the knots.

The sheet-rope was strong thanks to Charlie, who had showed them how to make knots on their sailing excursion to the cave. Little did they know it would come in handy so soon.

Keoni tied the sheet-rope around the leg of the solid wood dresser that sat next to the window. "It'll hold," confirmed Leilani, tugging on the lifeline to test its strength.

"We've gotta make sure the coast is clear. All we need is for someone to see us dangling from the side of the house."

"We're just gonna have to take our chances . . . you first, *Brah*."

"I'll toss you for it," replied Keoni in the first playful moment they'd had since they'd been carried off the beach.

"Ah, we don't have any money."

"Oh, right. Okay then, rock-scissors-paper! Ready—set— go!"

"Rock smashes scissors. I win again!" boasted Leilani. "You first."

They gazed out the window into the backyard, its boundaries marked by a peach-colored stucco wall. Plantings of wine red *ti* and speckled crotons joined a mesh of climbing vines and slender Manila palms along the border. It looked like a lush mini-jungle, but tamed.

The small but well manicured lawn was not open to the ocean as one would expect, but enclosed by the unbroken bougainvillea hedge. From the beach, the house was completely hidden.

"Who would do that?" the twins asked. "Why would anyone block the way to the beach?" Beach access is prized among all island people.

A boost from Leilani, and Keoni hoisted himself onto the window ledge. With his hands clasping the sheet-rope stretched tight, his arms were steady as he prepared for his descent.

But he executed a ninja-like leap instead and landed silently on his tiptoes and fingertips back in the room. "It's too risky now, Lei. I think we should wait until dark."

Thirty

Johann was in a quandary. He had never given into an ultimatum before. It was completely against his principles to sing for Dr. Vile.

But Dr. Vile had thrown him a curve ball. Who were these fans of his? Could they be the kids he'd heard calling his name, the two kids Sonny said were carried away by Dr. Vile's henchmen?

Would Dr. Vile make good on his implied threat? Never before had Johann been subjected to blackmail.

If he did sacrifice his principles and obey Dr. Vile's command where was the guarantee he would be released? Dr. Vile hadn't mentioned that. Other demands, perhaps even more distasteful than this one, could be made.

If Johann refused to sing for his captor what would happen to the kids? Their fate was in his hands.

Johann's head was swimming, and the more he thought about the situation, the more agitated he became. Johann the Calm, Johann the Cool, Johann the Brave—Johann didn't feel he was any of these things.

Since his first encounter with Johann, Sonny had been

his constant companion. "It's not just that I feel safe when I'm with you, Mr. Johann," said Sonny, "but I like you too."

"And I like you, Sonny," responded Johann, "You are good company indeed."

It was not only the enormous difference in size that made theirs an unlikely friendship. Johann, though a citizen of the world and adored by many, was basically solitary, like all humpbacks. It wasn't easy for Johann to open up to Sonny. It took Sonny to break the ice.

"Mr. Johann, you look troubled. Would you like to talk about it?"

Thirty-one

"Good call, *Brah*," said Leilani. Better we stay till they bring us some food. Then they might not check on us for a while."

"Okay with me. Besides, I'm getting hungry. *Shoots*, wish we didn't have to see the big man again though. He gives me the creeps."

On cue, familiar footsteps approached the room.

"Quick, Keoni!" Leilani cried, no longer mindful of speaking in a whisper. Their sheet-rope was still tied to the leg of the dresser!

What a strong and complicated knot they'd created. Keoni's fingers fumbled. The steps grew closer. "Hurry!" urged Leilani, glancing nervously over her shoulder at the bedroom door. Just as the key turned in the lock, the knot came undone. Leilani grabbed the sheet-rope and scrambled under the bed as the door swung open.

Sure enough, there stood the big man, intimidating even with a tray in his hands like a waiter. On it were two Styrofoam cartons stacked one on top of the other along with large paper cups of soda.

"Where's your sister?" boomed the big man, his glaring eyes sweeping the room.

"She's . . . ah, hi-hiding under the bed, mister, 'cause she's, she's scared. Come out, Leilani, it's okay," stammered Keoni, thinking fast.

It didn't take much for Leilani to pretend to be frightened. That was a close call. Her heart was beating like a hummingbird's wings.

Leilani emerged from her hiding place, trembling. The big man, satisfied that all was well, turned and left, locking the door behind him.

"Man, it's a good thing we didn't try to leave. They would've nailed us," said Keoni. "I wonder if he'll come back for this tray tonight."

"*Shoots*, he might. Now what'll we do?"

"Let's eat first. We'll think better after we've had some *grinds*."

The ordinary looking take-out cartons gave no hint as to what was inside. Chopsticks in paper wrappers and plastic packets of *shoyu* on the tray were another story though, clues that their meal would be something more appetizing than overcooked burgers and cold French fries.

Yes!—a *plate lunch* of *chicken katsu* on a bed of grated cabbage with "two scoops rice" and macaroni salad, island style. The twins devoured every last morsel. Maybe it wasn't as good as Auntie Pua's *katsu*, but, never mind, it hit the spot.

"Don't get too comfortable. We have to figure out what we're gonna do," said Leilani. She felt like taking a nap after the adult-size meal.

Keoni's eyes narrowed. "Got it, Lei," he said in a whisper, still worried that the room could be bugged. He picked up the tray and placed it on the table by the door. "That's so the big man won't have to come very far into the room if he comes back for it. Let's dim the lights and pile up pillows under the quilt so it looks like we're asleep." Leilani helped Keoni punch and fluff the down-filled pillows, sculpting them to look like their sleeping bodies. That part was fun, a brief break from their troubles.

"We should try to move the dresser closer to the window so the curtains will hide the rope," said Leilani.

It wasn't easy moving the heavy piece of furniture but they accomplished it together, inch by inch.

Trying to relax until the appointed hour, the twins watched the sun setting over the lagoon. The sight of the fiery ball sinking into the ocean eluded them though. The enormous wall blotted out the horizon.

Birds, oblivious to the twin's plight, chirped gaily, preparing for their nighttime rest. The sky turned mauve, then purple with streaks of orange. Finally darkness fell.

It was time.

Thirty-two

"It wasn't as bad as I thought," said Leilani after climbing down the homemade rope. The twins were used to climbing things, just not that high. They once helped Uncle Kalani craft a ladder for their tree house from bamboo that grew on the edge of their backyard. Mainly the ladder was for Auntie Pua to use. The twins thought it was more fun to climb up and down the vines hanging from the Banyan tree that held the little house in its arms.

"We're landlocked," said Keoni.

"So let's check out what's around the house," said Leilani. Her eyes were alert as she looked left, then right, barely moving her head as if any movement might give them away. A moment's pause and a couple of deep breaths later, the two skirted the corner. There before them was a large window illuminated from inside by a crystal chandelier.

A massive dining room table covered with gold-rimmed china and snowy white linen was set for an elegant dinner. Polished silver and gleaming glassware sparkled under teardrop crystals suspended from above. A porcelain vase held a lavish centerpiece of tropical flowers, the profusion of reds and pinks flanked by tapered white candles waiting to be lit. The scene was a far cry from their fondly remembered birthday *luau*.

Through another window they were able to see into the adjoining room. A dozen or so people stood around in formal dress. The women wore long gowns and were adorned with jewels, and the men were in tuxedos. They had never seen anything like it outside of the movies.

Sure, people got dressed up in Hawaii but that usually meant wearing *aloha* shirts and *muumuu* in colorful Hawaiian prints. A beautiful *lei* of flowers, shells or *kukui* nuts would provide the final touch. In honor of such a dressy occasion slippers might be replaced by shoes. Come to think of it, they had memories of Uilani's junior prom and the beautiful lavender gown Auntie Pua had made for her. She had gone with David, who wore a tuxedo rented from Gilbert's in Wailuku. Instead of a bow tie he donned a *maile* lei, bringing the fresh scent of the forest with him.

They had never seen anyone get so dressed up just to eat before.

They crouched transfixed outside the window. Waiters in short white jackets and black pants with shiny stripes down the sides were passing out *pupu* on little silver trays. The twins cautiously moved closer to the window.

The murmur of low voices was broken by the chiming of a grandfather clock that stood in a far corner of the stately room. It would have been at home in a museum with its ornately carved wood and Roman numerals in shining gold. The polished brass pendulum was swinging behind etched glass. It chimed seven times.

Everyone in the room stood motionless. Then came a sound, the most entrancing sound one could ever hope to hear. It was Johann, singing. The guests stood spellbound and so did the twins.

Johann could sing just about anything—arias in Italian, jazz, blues and pop, Hawaiian *mele,* even Inuit. But tonight he sang in Whale. The haunting, otherworldly sounds seemed to come from the beginning of time.

"Wow," whispered Leilani.

"Awesome," Keoni whispered back. " Do you think they have microphones in the lagoon?"

The unexpected private concert by Johann Sebastian Humpbach was a huge hit with Dr. Vile's distinguished guests, potential investors in a new business venture. They chatted cheerfully as they were ushered to their seats at the exquisitely laid table, talking of nothing but Johann's music.

The host sat at the head of the table but his back was toward the twins, so they couldn't see his face. He stood and proposed a toast to his guests and his new *partner* Johann. Glasses of champagne clinked. The guests nodded their heads in approval.

Thirty-three

Mrs. Witherspoon's office was deemed safe to use again. The media had decamped and were off to greener pastures. Auntie Pua, Uncle Kalani, Mrs. Witherspoon and Captain Kenny were discouraged and frustrated by the lack of progress.

Mrs. Witherspoon had hung Johann's star-spangled scarf on the wall behind her desk, hoping it would provide them with much needed inspiration. Draped from corner to corner, the scarf's metallic fringe cascaded down the sides of the wall like a waterfall.

Sitting in front of the glimmering backdrop Auntie Pua asked, "If there was a giant lava wall concealing a lagoon, could it be seen against the lava flow? I mean, would it blend in with the other rock?"

"It's possible," said the captain. "I know of a pond called the 'fishbowl' and it's just like that. If you didn't know where the entrance was, you wouldn't notice it, it's so well hidden. But believe me," he said, "we've searched everywhere."

"Please don't misunderstand," Auntie Pua said in a soft voice, "I know you're doing your best. I'm just trying to explore all possibilities."

"I know, Pua, I know. It's just so mind-boggling. I've been sailing these waters for over thirty years . . . "

"Okay, everybody, let's get it together," commanded a stern Clara Witherspoon, clapping her hands twice. "All negativity out the door. Bye-bye. It's gone now.

"We'll find the twins. It's just a matter of time. Where were they when they disappeared? At the mouth of that cave! It's got to have something to do with that cave!" she said, snapping her fingers for emphasis.

"Clara, the Coast Guard scuba divers searched the cave thoroughly. They hit a dead-end," reminded Captain Kenny.

"Isn't that odd, Captain? I mean a lava cave is a lava tube. Why would it suddenly be blocked at the end?" asked Mrs. Witherspoon.

"Well, gee, I don't know, Clara," said the captain stroking his chin. "I have a geologist friend I can check with."

Thirty-four

While the twins' kidnapper and his well-heeled guests were being served dinner by an army of waiters, Keoni and Leilani decided to explore the rest of the grounds. The whole place was boxed-in by the peach stucco wall except on the bougainvillea side. The only opening was an elaborately sculpted metal gate that guarded the entrance. It was closed and in plain view.

A white stretch limousine with dark-tinted windows sat in the circular driveway. A chauffeur stood nearby. If the twins had entertained the idea of appealing to him for help, that thought quickly vanished when the big man approached the driver and engaged him in friendly conversation.

With the front blocked, the fugitives reversed course. They retraced their steps, past the lit windows with the dinner party in progress, past the homemade rope partially hidden by a profusion of plants.

Keoni and Leilani darted across the grass and began scaling the maze of vines and foliage that climbed the wall. "Piece of cake," said Keoni, just as motion sensor lights bathed the yard in a sea of light.

Agitated voices seemed to come from all directions. The twins froze in their tracks.

Was there time to finish climbing the wall? They couldn't just vault over the top without scoping it out first. What if bougainvillea with its thorns that could puncture a tire or razor sharp lava were on the other side?

Seeming to read each other's minds the twins hopped back down to the ground and sprinted to the house. They flattened themselves against a wall behind a large, fan-shaped traveler's palm. "Please, please, don't let them find us," prayed Leilani.

"And don't let them find the rope," added Keoni. They remained in their hiding place, petrified.

The big man, along with the chauffeur and two other men the twins had not seen before, advanced into the backyard all the way to the bougainvillea. Finding nothing, they hastened back toward the house. The big man and the chauffeur stopped in front of the traveler's palm that served as the twins' camouflage.

"Nobody here. Must've been a rat that set it off," said the big man. "Better make our patrols every twenty minutes, just in case. The boss won't be happy if anything interferes with entertaining his guests."

The big man punctuated his remarks by throwing the cigarette that had been dangling from the corner of his mouth onto the ground with a flourish and grinding it into the dirt with the heel of his shoe.

His associate dutifully picked the butt up after him.

Thirty-five

"Uh-huh, uh-huh," murmured Captain Kenny seeming to hang on every word coming from the telephone. The gang sat in rapt silence as the captain, sitting on a corner of Mrs. Witherspoon's desk, continued his conversation with Kehau, the Park Service geologist who worked at Haleakala National Park.

They were all on the edges of their seats waiting to hear what the geologist had to say about lava tubes. The moment Captain Kenny hung up, Mrs. Witherspoon blurted out, "What did she say? Tell us everything!"

"She said blocked lava tubes are not uncommon and are usually the result of cave-ins caused by earthquakes—we have more earthquakes than most people realize. Sometimes a new lava flow rumbling over the old one can cause a tube to collapse. The result is a blockage, a jumble of rocks."

"Didn't the divers say they found a dead-end of smooth rock?" asked Uncle Kalani.

"That's right," said the captain.

"Kehau also said that even if a new lava flow cascaded over the collapsed rocks like a waterfall and coated them with *pahoehoe*— that's the smooth flowing, less gaseous lava that looks like taffy hardened up—it would still have bumps in it. And though theoretically possible, the occurrence would be rare."

"There must be a written report of the Coast Guard's findings. Maybe there's a description of the cave's dead-end," said Auntie Pua.

"Good point, Pua. I'll call the Coast Guard," said the captain, dialing the number he'd memorized years ago. When he hung up he said, "The report states that the divers came upon a dead-end. There's no further description. I guess we should interview the divers."

Reading the trio of faces, he added, "I know you're anxious, but it could take a while to track these guys down. They're not going to be sitting by a phone. I promise I'll get back to you as soon as I know something."

It was hard to investigate anything with Clara Witherspoon breathing down his neck. He'd do much better without everyone looking on. He missed the privacy and familiarity of his own office and he wanted to make his inquiries from there.

Auntie Pua and Uncle Kalani thought it was a reasonable notion but Mrs. Witherspoon was less understanding. She wanted the next step to commence immediately, preferably with her present.

Finally, in the interest of harmony, she relented.

Thirty-six

Even after the big man and the chauffeur had moved on, Keoni and Leilani stood still as stone. Leilani broke the silence and whispered in her brother's ear, "That was scary. Did you hear what they said? They'll be back in twenty minutes."

"We can't climb the wall again. We'll set off the lights. The way to the beach is blocked by the *boug* and we don't know how to get through it," said Keoni. "I know this sounds weird, but I think I saw the hedge move when the big man carried me off the beach. We need to check out the hedge, but if we try to cross the yard again that'll set off the sensors too."

"Even if we did find our way through the hedge we'd be back on the beach with nowhere to hide. Then what?" asked Leilani. "But if we stay here we might not be so lucky next time."

This game of hide-and-seek was about as much fun as swimming with a school of jellyfish.

"Maybe we could try climbing up the rope, back to the room, and . . . never mind," said Leilani, withdrawing her suggestion. "Sorry, bad idea."

"Wait a minute, Lei, maybe you're right. We might be better off hiding inside, at least till we figure out what to do." Keoni pointed, "Look over your shoulder, to the left."

There above her was a dark, open window, the curtains inside fluttering in the evening breeze. "What about the screen?" asked Leilani.

"Help me find a sharp rock that'll fit in my hand. I'll try to cut a hole in it."

"You can use my hands as a step," said Leilani, wasting no time in knitting her fingers together. Keoni found a suitable stone and used her entwined hands as a launching pad. With his legs dangling next to his sister's head, he hung from the first floor window ledge with both hands, the stone in his pocket. Leilani moved directly under the window so Keoni could plant his feet on her shoulders.

Leilani braced herself by widening her stance and flattening the palms of her hands against the side of the house, her arms steady and strong.

Balancing himself with one hand, Keoni sawed away at the screen with the other. The small stone with its pointed edge was the perfect tool.

The sun baked this side of the house much of the day, and over time the screen had become weak. It stretched easily under Keoni's assault, and he was able to create a tear in the mesh. He dropped the rock to the ground with a soft thud and put his hand through the screen giving it a good yank. He ripped a hole big enough to crawl through.

Straddling the windowsill, Keoni could feel the brittle

mesh scratch his skin. He drew in his outside leg, doing his best to avoid the screen's sharp edges.

Safely inside on tiptoes, Keoni leaned out the window through the gaping hole. "Okay, Sis, hurry. They could be back any minute."

Leilani spotted a good-sized *pohoku* nearby. Using all her strength, she rolled the large rock underneath the window. By standing on it she was able to grasp Keoni's outstretched arms.

"Try to grab the windowsill when you get up high enough. Ready— set—go!"

Keoni pulled as hard as he could and Leilani grabbed the windowsill on the first try. He clasped her arms as she swung a leg onto the sill and straddled the ledge like Keoni had done before her. She paused for a moment to catch her breath before swinging the other leg in, landing feet first through the window.

No sooner had Leilani landed on the floor inside the dark room when the floodlights outside blazed on again, this time set off by Dr. Vile's men who were making their rounds.

"Close call," *Sistah*.

"So what else is new, *Brah*?" she replied.

Thirty-seven

It took awhile for their eyes to adjust. They couldn't see much, but the window's plain curtains hinted at the room's practical nature. It appeared to be used for storage. The twins groped their way toward the dim light that seeped under the door.

Leilani found the light switch, but she hesitated to turn it on without consulting Keoni. "What if someone walks by and sees the light?"

"Maybe we could turn it on and off real quick, just to see where we are," said Keoni.

Leilani flicked the light on and off, pausing long enough to scan the room. "It's dive city!" exclaimed Keoni, impressed. Wet suits and buoyancy control devices known as BCD's were suspended on hangers, along with gauges and regulators. Masks and snorkels dangled from wooden pegs. Fins, weight belts, and gloves were stacked on shelves, and several tanks of air sat on the floor in the corner.

"I wish Uncle Kalani was here to see this . . . " said Keoni. "*Shoots*, Lei! We missed our last diving certification class. And our written exam. I hope the YMCA will let us make it up. They were going to show us another video too."

"Yeah, and we were supposed to have our pictures taken for our dive cards," remembered Leilani. "Nothing we can do about it now."

"This looks like a pretty safe place to be for the moment. I doubt anyone will be going diving tonight," said Keoni. "Anyway, those guys don't look like divers. They look like big city thugs."

"You know what? I've had enough excitement for one night. Can we just chill?" said Leilani, sitting down on the floor. Keoni joined his sister on the cold tile.

"Did those guys call their boss Dr. Vile?" asked Leilani.

"That's what I heard. Dr. Vile. What did he mean when he said Johann was his *partner*? I don't believe it."

Footsteps came and went as the dinner party ended and the staff began to clean up. It was hours before activity ceased. Through the open window they heard the limousine depart with the last of Dr. Vile's guests. The house grew still.

So far, so good. They wondered if anyone had checked on them in the room upstairs. If so, their ruse had worked. If they had been found out, surely there would have been a commotion. How long did they have before someone discovered the truth?

"*Shoots*, I wish we had Auntie Pua's cell phone," muttered Leilani.

"That's it! Let's see if we can find a phone! Bet there are lots of phones in this house. Sounds like everyone's asleep. If we're gonna do it, we should do it now."

Leilani opened the door a crack, then wider, and poked her head out into the hallway "Right or left, Keoni, your call. You were down here before."

Keoni slipped past his sister into the hall and looked both ways. "Well, we know the dining room is on the same side as the kitchen and the back stair is that way," he said pointing. "That's the pantry door and the room at the end is where Dr. Vile spoke to me. I didn't see a phone in there."

"So let's check out the kitchen. Go," said Leilani, giving Keoni a little shove.

The twins moved noiselessly down the hall to the kitchen. The door was open and a night light was on by the sink. Curiously, there was no phone.

They left the kitchen through a different door, past the dining room where all evidence of the party was gone except for the floral centerpiece on the table. Silently, they continued to explore the downstairs, but still couldn't find a phone. "Maybe they only use cell phones," said Leilani.

"Hope not," said Keoni, "keep looking." There was one room left to explore and the twins, becoming bolder, weren't about to ignore it just because the door was closed.

They listened at the door for voices and then furtively entered the room. What they saw was not what they had expected. The room was not dark. The recessed ceiling lights were on, and so was a chrome desk lamp. Electronic equipment with its pinpoints of light in red, green and orange lined the walls. A table microphone sat on a sleek *koa* desk, and a workstation housed several computers with their monitors aglow.

The room was a startling contrast to the rest of the house. Keoni and Leilani started to snoop around.

"Look, Lei, a phone!"

Before Keoni could reach the cell phone that had been left on the black leather sofa, they heard the sound of voices and footsteps.

"Hide!" they exclaimed in hushed tones as they scurried about, looking for a suitable place to secret themselves. Leilani opened the door to an over-sized *koa* cabinet with woven cane panels in the doors. The top half held a large-screened TV, but the bottom half was empty.

Keoni and Leilani would have to scrunch themselves up into a ball to fit inside.

So they did.

Thirty-eight

The twins were becoming adept at slow, quiet breathing. Not only had it helped them remain undetected but it served to calm them down in the harrowing situations they'd been finding themselves lately.

They didn't dare move their heads to try and see out the small *puka* in the weave of the doors. They were so close to their captors, the slightest movement or sound was dangerous. But they could hear just fine.

When the door opened they were surprised at all the shuffling about, not expecting so many feet to enter the room. A conversation with a mix of voices ensued, with Dr. Vile, a.k.a. *the voice*, obviously in charge.

"I think the evening went rather well. My compliments to the chef. Johann was superb and the investors were suitably impressed. I do believe they're all on board."

Dr. Vile directed the next subject to one person in particular, perhaps the big man. "Have you checked on those kids?" *the voice* asked.

"Yeah, I was up there an hour ago, boss. They were sound asleep."

"Good. They're turning out to be very useful. Without them as leverage it would have been difficult getting Johann to perform. Now that the investors think we have Johann's full cooperation, as witnessed by his singing at my dinner party, we shall, in a short time, become very wealthy men."

"You're already wealthy, boss," said a brazen henchman, causing the others to chuckle nervously.

"Yes, of course. But this is sheer genius, if I do say so myself. It's been a delightful challenge and everything is going according to plan and more. The twins were the perfect gift, insurance for Johann's continued cooperation."

"I must thank you for opening the entrance to the lagoon at just the right moment, even though it was accidental, Yado. Of course if it ever happens again, I won't be quite so forgiving," said Dr. Vile, his sinister intent made very clear.

"Yes, sir," replied the underling in a timid voice.

"Now, let's see if we picked up anything this afternoon. Play the tape back for me, Yado," ordered Dr. Vile.

Keeping quiet lest they give away their presence in this den of scoundrels was agony for the twins. Yet they restrained themselves, and listened.

It was hard not to poke each other when Keoni and Leilani heard the recorded voices of Uncle Kalani and Auntie Pua, Mrs. Witherspoon and Captain Kenny, too.

The sound of their auntie and uncle's voices filled them with hope. Their guardians were applauding Johann's scarf being displayed on Mrs. Witherspoon's office wall. Captain Kenny and Uncle Kalani reminisced about the day the twins had dragged it out of the water.

The conversation continued and the twins hung on every word. They savored the connection to their *ohana* that had been so unexpectedly given them. The voices faded away but the twins knew that their auntie and uncle had not given up and neither had the others!

“It seems as though we have some tenacious busy-bodies about to investigate the cave. This complicates things,” Dr. Vile growled. “Time is of the essence—we don’t want any uninvited guests at our recording session.

“We never assumed this enterprise would be without its challenges, gentlemen. Let’s proceed as planned, though with an accelerated schedule. With Johann’s scarf hanging on the wall of their meeting place, we’ll hear their every word. We shall be well advised of their plans and progress so we can rest assured there won’t be any surprises.”

Dr. Vile’s mood improved as he congratulated himself on his genius, the inventing of a special scarf, its properties allowing it to emerge from the sea unscathed. Not only was it made beautiful with its twinkling stars, but those glistening appliqués in silver and gold were actually mini-microphones and transmitters in disguise.

When he had given the scarf to Johann as a gift, anonymously of course, the idea was to be able to record his every sound and package his music to sell to his adoring fans. A monopoly was all but guaranteed. After Dr. Vile got what he was after, Johann could have a serious accident, perhaps a collision with a ship. Unfortunately, Dr. Vile and his cronies had overlooked one thing. Neither Johann nor his brethren sang when they were in Alaska. They only sang in Hawaii where it was too warm for Johann to wear his scarf. He had traded it in for the *kukui nut lei.*

That's when Dr. Vile constructed the fortress-like wall around the lagoon, installing microphones and loudspeakers. The entire sound system worked beautifully. It had been a huge investment, but nothing compared to the hundreds of millions he stood to make as the sole source of Johann's music throughout the world. Ultimately, Dr. Vile would have very little of his own fortune invested in the project. All costs would be covered by the promised contributions of his investors.

And though the scarf had not worked as Dr. Vile planned, it still served a useful purpose, thus affirming another of his favorite mottoes, "Shoot for the stars and you might hit the moon."

Yes, everything was going extremely well. He was going to be very, very rich. Obscenely rich. And very, very powerful, thanks to Johann.

Thirty-nine

Nothing exhilarated Johann like singing. Despite his initial repugnance at being blackmailed into performing for Dr. Vile, Johann sang like he always did, with all his heart.

Johann could be naive. He was such a good soul that it was hard for him to conceive of anyone having *no* redeeming qualities. Johann thought his music might bring out some latent goodness in these unscrupulous men. Perhaps they would mend their wicked ways.

They *were* entranced by the music, but it had no lasting effect on their character. Not a smidgen. Not one iota. It had put Dr. Vile in a good mood, but it hadn't changed him. Nothing would.

In fact, it served to whet his appetite even more and reinforce the notion that he was on the right path to cornering the market in all things Johann. Dr. Vile had big plans.

"Mr. Humpbach, can you hear me?" said Dr. Vile into the microphone. "Your performance was magnificent—my congratulations and thank you for your cooperation."

Cooperation? thought Johann. *This guy sure has a lot of nerve.*

"I'd like to propose a business deal, Mr. Humpbach. I want to record a compilation of your music. I have a state-of-the-art sound system here with the capability of creating recordings of the highest quality, using the finest talent available. Your music can be everywhere in the world, even when you can't be. Wouldn't that be a wonderful gift?"

This was not the first time Johann had been approached to enter into a deal to record his music, although this was the only time under duress. He had granted permission on several occasions to environmental groups, scholarship funds, and the like. His music was always given freely, for Johann had no use for money.

Johann didn't mind if enterprising folks like Captain Kenny made a few bucks. The captain performed a service and did it well. It had always been like that. It was Johann's way of spreading the wealth.

But Johann would never agree to anyone monopolizing his music. Certainly not someone like Dr. Vile.

"Kidnapping fish for profit and smashing up the reef! Indeed!" said Johann.

"Yes, I'm sorry about that, Mr. Humpbach. Some of my men got a bit carried away. Wanted to make a little money on the side. I've already taken steps to punish those responsible. I can assure you it won't happen again.

"I am prepared to compensate you very well, Mr. Humpbach. You can take your portion of the proceeds and donate them to your favorite charity. I will handle everything for you. You can be a force for good in the world," said Dr. Vile, smooth as a silver-tongued snake.

A part of Johann wanted to believe Dr. Vile. Maybe he wasn't so bad after all . . .

If Johann had a lapse in judgment, it didn't last long, thanks to Sonny who whispered in his ear, "Don't buy it, Mr. Johann. He can't be trusted, believe me."

"I have no intention of going into business with you, Dr. Vile. And I would like to be released. I've been detained long enough. Let those children go too. That was the deal. I sang. Now free the kids."

"I'm sorry if you got the impression I would release the children if you sang, Mr. Humpbach. You misunderstood. I gave you no such guarantee.

"I'm afraid you have no choice in the matter if you and the children ever wish to get out of here. The recording session will commence first thing tomorrow. I expect you to be ready and willing.

"Goodnight, Mr. Humpbach. Sleep well," said Dr. Vile, ending the conversation and switching off the microphone.

"Are you really gonna let'm go, boss?" The voice belonged to the big man.

"Never! The Johann Sebastian Humpbach Whale Song Tour is officially dead in the water. He will record for me and me alone! And . . . ur . . . for your benefit of course, gentlemen. You have a lot to gain."

"What'll you do come spring, Dr. Vile?" another of the men asked. "You don't have to feed Johann now, but by spring he'll be getting mighty hungry and the only place that has enough krill is Alaska. If he doesn't return to Alaska, he'll starve."

"That's not a problem," responded Dr. Vile. "By then, we'll

have made all the recordings we need. We can release them a few at a time. We'll have enough music to last for years! As far as Johann is concerned, who cares? If he croaks, so what? We'll be long gone."

Keoni and Leilani shuddered when they heard Dr. Vile's cold words. How could anybody be so rotten? They had to warn Johann!

"Please maintain the surveillance around the house. Even though it's impossible for anyone to see Johann through the hedge should they get on to the property, there's no point in taking any chances. We have a lot at stake and I don't want anything to go wrong. Tomorrow is going to be a big day."

"I have one more call to make, and then I'm off to bed. Goodnight, gentlemen," said Dr. Vile as he walked out of the room, phone in hand.

Forty

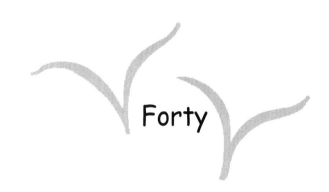

Keoni and Leilani listened intently as Dr. Vile's inner circle waited for him to leave the room before following him out the door. The twins were tuned to every word, every footstep, every sound. Leilani burst out of the cabinet like a gust of Kona wind the minute she heard the door close.

"*Shoots*, Lei, what if one of them comes back for something? Don't you think we should've given it a minute or two?" scolded Keoni, emerging slowly from the cubbyhole beneath the TV.

"Sorry, Keoni. I couldn't stand it anymore. *Shoots*," she said, "he took the phone . . . "Leilani's voice trailed off as she made a beeline for the *koa* desk. "Dr. Vile must've spoken to Johann through this mike. I'll bet that's how he spoke to you in that little room."

"There must be several channels for this mike, Lei. Let's hope Dr. Vile left it on the one to the lagoon and not one of the rooms. I'll bet they're all wired."

Leilani switched on the microphone and took a deep breath. "Here goes."

They looked at each other, what they were about to do

sinking in. Leilani switched off the microphone so they could formulate a plan.

"What should we say to Johann . . . exactly? I mean, we don't have much time," said Leilani.

"Yeah, and what are we gonna do after we talk to him? Do you think we'll be able to hear him too?"

"Maybe. We heard Johann talk to Dr. Vile through those speakers. I wonder if another switch needs to be turned on."

"What if our voices get sent through the house? Then what?" said Keoni.

"We gotta decide," said Leilani. "The big man is going to be suspicious when he brings breakfast to our room and we're still not up."

"I vote for using the mike. Odds are pretty good Dr. Vile kept it on the channel to the lagoon," said Keoni.

"Yeah. And even if we can't hear Johann at least we can warn him about Dr. Vile's plans."

Leilani switched on the microphone once again. There was to be no test run, no sound check. This was the moment of truth. "Mr. Humpbach," she began, "this is Leilani, you don't know me but . . . "

Leilani explained all that happened—their snorkeling expedition and finding Johann's scarf, their return to the cave in search of clues and being sucked through the whirling muck, their capture on the beach.

Keoni took over and told Johann about Dr. Vile's plans and his fate if he didn't escape from the lagoon.

They talked longer than they intended. Had their voices been piped through the house, Dr. Vile's men would have been on them by now.

The twins were disappointed when they didn't hear back from Johann. They were about to give up when a melodious voice boomed from the speakers overhead as if it came from the heavens. "This is Johann and I heard everything you said.

"Now it all makes sense, the kidnappings, my imprisonment, Dr. Vile's demands," he said. "*Mahalo* for the warning. I'm so sorry you were placed in such *pilikia* on my account. It's terrible, just terrible."

"Oh no, sir," said Keoni in awe at speaking with the great Johann Sebastian Humpbach. "It was Dr. Vile's greed that started it all. Don't blame yourself."

"That's right, said Leilani. "Keoni and I wanted to find you, but we were in it for the adventure too. We got ourselves into this mess. The point is, what do we do now?"

Forty-one

Despite searching the deepest recesses of his brain, Johann had no recollection of how he ended up in the lagoon. He and the twins compared notes, trying to figure out how they got there.

"I don't remember a cave but I do remember the cold, the shivering, the darkness—then suddenly the light," said Johann. "It could have been the drugs wearing off. Or maybe it was the tunnel."

Keoni and Leilani had both been in the mouth of the cave when the underwater tornado hit. They had vivid memories of being stung by the swirling sediment in the water but nothing after that until they washed up on the beach.

Keoni told Johann about overhearing the conversation in Mrs. Witherspoon's office and how it was transmitted by the metallic stars on Johann's scarf. Johann recalled how delighted he had been to receive such a beautiful gift. It had become his trademark because he wore it all the time, except in Hawaii, where it was too warm.

They concluded that all arrows pointed in the same direction—to the cave. They decided that Johann should swim around the perimeter of the lagoon and search for an underwater cavern while the twins stayed in contact at command central.

Johann found no opening whatsoever.

“Mr. Humpbach, could you please look again, this time focusing on the west side of the lagoon, that’s where Leilani and I washed ashore.”

“Please, call me Johann.”

The determined whale, with Sonny struggling to keep up, conducted a more thorough search of the lagoon’s west end.

“Hmm. That’s curious.”

“What is, Mr. Humpbach, ur, I mean, Johann?”

“There seems to be a sort of giant boulder resting on a rocky shelf. It’s huge. My size. The entire wall is made up of giant boulders. This one is different though. It bumps out, it’s not level with the rest of the rocks. And it appears to be almost a perfect square, like it was chiseled.”

“Look at this,” said Sonny, examining something strange under the boulder. Though he didn’t know what they were, Sonny described what sounded to Keoni and Leilani like tracks.

“Wait a minute,” recalled Leilani. What did Dr. Vile say to one of the guys, Yado, I think? Something about messing up and opening the entrance to the lagoon? Remember, Keoni? Try to remember,” urged Leilani.

“Yeah, he said don’t let it happen again, but that it was good that it did because it brought us to him! I forgot about that. There must be a way into the lagoon that opens and closes. Dr. Vile said so!”

“It sounds like this could be it,” said Johann. “Now, if

we only knew how to open it . . . "

"Maybe the controls are in this room. Give us a minute and we'll look around," said Leilani.

Keoni and Leilani carefully examined each piece of equipment. From their visits to the recording studio with Uncle Kawika and *Nalu*, they recognized much of it as being used for recording music. Then there were computers, printers, monitors, speakers and of course the big TV. Hold on, what was that big lever that looked like a hockey stick jutting from the floor? It was embedded in a metal plate with a slot on either side so it could be moved back and forth.

"This could be it, Johann," said Keoni, growing more comfortable in calling the great whale by his first name. "Ready to give it a try?"

"Give me and Sonny here a chance to back off a bit, just in case," said Johann.

The lever was stiff and not easy to move. It was clear that it would take both brother and sister to accomplish the task. "Okay. Ready— set— go!"

It took all their might but the lever moved the foot or so to the end of the slot. "What happened, Johann?" they chorused. "Did it move? Johann, Johann, are you there?"

Even though Sonny and Johann swam away from the boulder as a precaution, when the giant rock moved, the resulting change in water pressure created a tempest. The water from the ocean outside the wall surged through the tube like a flash flood in a desert gulch. Johann with his gigantic size was able to weather the storm but poor little Sonny blew past him like he was shot from a cannon and didn't stop until he smashed into the reef.

"Sonny, Sonny, are you okay?" said the worried Johann finding Sonny collapsed on the seafloor. There was a squeaky moan as the tiny squid slowly opened his eyes.

"I think I'm okay, Mr. Johann," said Sonny, although he looked a bit battered. Johann tenderly scooped him up with his flipper. Sonny was touched by this gesture of concern.

"Leilani, Keoni!" Johann exclaimed. "It's open, the cave's open! Now I know how you got here. You must've gotten caught in the rush of seawater. You were sucked through the tube when the rock was accidentally moved. It's calmed down now. I think I can swim through the cave. It might be tight, but . . . "

"Oh no! Someone's coming!" were the last words Johann heard before the microphone went dead.

Forty-two

The intruders had no choice but to return to their hiding place inside the TV cabinet. They couldn't take a chance and make a break for the scuba room with footsteps fast approaching. Fortunately, their confinement was brief, for whoever entered the room came and left immediately, as if retrieving something previously forgotten.

"You know what," said Keoni, "we're pushing our luck. We need to *hele* on!"

Leilani agreed. "Yeah. There's nothing more to do here."

As soon as the footsteps faded, the twins bolted from the cabinet and made a dash for the door. Keoni opened it a crack, checking the passageway in both directions. In hushed tones he said, "Now, Lei! Go!"

Silently the twosome sprinted side-by-side down the hallway like *Menehune* scampering through the forest at night and made their way back to their safe haven, the scuba room.

They felt oddly comfortable there among all the neoprene and couldn't resist the urge to check out the gear again. Leilani removed a wetsuit from a hanger and bunched it up against the base of the door so they could turn on the light without the glow escaping.

"Wow, it's way better than I thought. There's all kinds of stuff in here. Dr. Vile must be really rich," marveled Keoni.

"Whoa. What is that?" Leilani pointed to a weird contraption hanging from a peg on the wall. It had straps and loops and was made out of nylon, stained with saltwater.

"It looks like a huge harness, maybe for a horse or something . . . hmm, no horse is that big. *Shoots*, it's big enough to lasso a whale," said Keoni examining the odd object more closely.

"It's Johann's size!" Leilani exclaimed. "Wow! Divers could have used this to tow Johann through the cave while he was knocked out."

"All the pieces of the puzzle are coming together," said Keoni.

Out of nowhere, a siren erupted—blaring, insistent, and wailing non-stop. The twins knew that whining sound. They had heard it many times before, usually on the first of every month, exactly at noon, the time of the regular monthly test. But this was not a test. The Pacific Tsunami Warning System was never tested in the middle of the night.

The sound was not foreign to Johann either. He knew it heralded danger but this wasn't his only clue, for Johann's ultra-sensitive, low frequency hearing could detect even the slightest change in the sea. He could sense that something huge was coming.

Now that the portal to the cave was open, Johann could flee this danger zone. He was free to go, thanks to the twins.

Free! He had been imprisoned. His very existence had been in danger. Now he was to have his life back.

But he couldn't leave Keoni and Leilani in this perilous place. He must be sure they were safe. He knew a tsunami could flood up to a thousand feet inland, its retreating waters washing everything in its path out to sea.

Johann gazed at the yawning mouth of the cavern. He could go for help, but there was no telling how long it would take to find anyone. By then it could be too late. Tsunamis travel at over five hundred miles an hour, the speed of a jet plane.

It wasn't just the twins that he felt responsible for. All the creatures of the reef were vulnerable to a tsunami striking the shore. They must be warned. A rapid withdrawal of the ocean would precede the tsunami's arrival, leaving the reef exposed. If Johann's newfound friends didn't get out of the lagoon they'd be left gasping, their bodies flopping in the sopping sand, hammered to smithereens by the onslaught of giant, crashing waves.

Once the sea receded, they'd have twenty minutes or so until the great wall of black water hit. Johann understood that many tsunami-related deaths happened when the sea floor was exposed and the curious drew near to see the reef, not knowing a tsunami was on the way.

As a tsunami crossed the deep ocean it wouldn't be felt by ships at sea and was invisible from the air. Its length from crest to crest could be a hundred miles or more. Its height from crest to trough just a few feet or less, so it looked like an ordinary wind-driven wave.

Trouble would start when the tsunami entered shallow

water. The speed would slow down and waves would start piling up on each other, building a tower of waves. A large tsunami could reach a height of over a hundred feet by the time it hit the shallows. The force would be devastating.

Johann took one last look at the mouth of the cave then turned around, swimming toward the reef. "Hurry, *wikiwiki*! Get out of the lagoon. Get out now! Big wave coming!"

Forty-three

The house seemed to come alive. Loud footsteps ran to and fro. It sounded like a fire drill in progress. Doors slammed and voices bounced off the walls. The commotion continued non-stop as Keoni and Leilani listened with their ears plastered to the door.

The footsteps receded and did not return. The house became as quiet as a museum closed on Mondays. Keoni and Leilani could hear the roar of an engine as the limousine drove away.

"It sounds like everyone's gone!" exclaimed Leilani.

"It's dead quiet. Why would they just take off like that and leave us?" asked Keoni.

"Who knows? Let's get back to the command post."

The twins ran through the house, checking the rooms for signs of life. The door to the communications room was open! They waited cautiously for a moment, their bodies flattened against the wall. Leilani peered around the corner. The whole place seemed to be deserted.

The twins ran into the vacated room. "Where is everything? All the computers and stuff are gone!" exclaimed Keoni.

Only the microphone was still in its place on the desk.

Leilani ran to the cabinet and turned on the TV. Even though it was the middle of the night, the twenty-four hour news would be on. She surfed through the channels with the remote that she had found on the leather couch.

"There it is, Channel 24." More tragedy in the Middle East. Floods in Wisconsin. Rolling blackouts in California. "C'mon, c'mon," she said, talking to the TV. "What about the tsunami warning in Hawaii?"

"I think I saw a radio in the kitchen," remembered Keoni. "If there's a local emergency, it'll be covered."

Keoni turned on the small, chrome-faced radio on the kitchen counter, zipping through the blur of music, listening for voices talking. He found a local Hawaiian music station where there was always a lot of chatter.

". . . and so, folks, that's one big tsunami coming. The earthquake south of the Aleutian Islands was one big *buggah*!" Then the station went to a commercial.

Keoni changed the channel, searching for more news of the earthquake. "It's a big story," said Leilani. "It should be on TV. Let's try again."

They returned to command central, not bothering to turn off the radio. The TV was still on too; some Hollywood couple was breaking up. Surprise, surprise.

If there was a giant earthquake it would be on Headline News eventually. They waited.

Finally it came, news of the earthquake near the Aleutian Islands with video footage of crumbling ice and avalanches. It was 7.6 on the Richter Scale, an earthquake of great magnitude. Fortunately the epicenter was in the middle of nowhere and no deaths were reported. But it was feared that the earthquake had spawned a tsunami that was headed for the Hawaiian Islands.

Uncle Oliver had told them the story of witnessing first-hand the destruction on the Big Island in 1946 when a huge tsunami hit. Though it was hard for the twins to imagine, he was a young man then, courting a girl who lived in Hilo on the eastern coast of the island. There had been no warning system in those days. The girl's father was dragged out to sea by a giant wave. Her distress was so great, she ended the romance.

Now seismographs detected tsunami-causing earthquakes. Water level changes were monitored at tidal gauge stations throughout the Pacific. All signs indicated a powerful tsunami was on its way. People were being evacuated from coastal areas. This was to be the first significant tsunami since 1964 when waves bulldozed onto the shore, snapping trees like twigs, toppling stonewalls, smashing houses, drowning the unwary.

Keoni and Leilani would not number themselves among the unwary. They had been warned.

The story was so fascinating that they forgot for the moment that it was not happening somewhere halfway around the world. It was happening in their own backyard and they were sitting ducks.

Forty-four

"Let's get outa here!"

The twins bounded from their places on the floor in front of the TV and headed for the front door.

"Wait a minute," remembered Keoni, "we need to get the dive lights from the scuba room." They detoured back to retrieve the lights, testing each one before deciding which to bring.

They dashed down the hall and bolted out the front door. The cinder road might lead to a neighbor to whom they could turn for help.

The security lights blinked on, illuminating the U-shaped driveway and decorative gate that guarded the entrance. The gate would be an easy climb with plenty of handholds and footholds in its curving forms.

Keoni was a few steps ahead of Leilani in their dash toward freedom. His outstretched arms were prepared to grab the gate and start climbing. He didn't want to waste a second.

"Stop, Keoni, stop!" screamed Leilani at the top of her lungs. Keoni slid to a halt just inches from the gate.

"What'd you yell at me for?"

Leilani pointed to a row of dead, giant cockroaches of the kind the twins called "747's" because they were so big. Sometimes they zoomed through the air, dive-bombing their unsuspecting targets. Now they were on their backs, in the dead-bug position, looking fried.

"The 747's are all dead," said Leilani. "What do you think killed 'em?"

"There's no time for this. C'mon, Lei, don't play games. What's up?"

"I think the gate might be electrified. I wouldn't put it past these crazy people."

Keoni reached down and picked up one of the three-inch-long cockroaches. He memorized every feature and then pitched it against the gate as if throwing a baseball.

Zap!

Keoni picked up the unfortunate creature and examined it again.

"It's fried, all right," confirmed Keoni. "These people *are lolo.* Someone could get killed!"

"I guess they wanted to make sure no one got onto the property while they were gone."

"Or maybe they didn't want anyone on the inside to get out," said Keoni, scowling. "Look's like it's gotta be the wall. Let's get the rope. We can use it to get down the other side."

"If I never see this place again it will be too soon," said Leilani. They went back into the house and took the stairs two at a time, up to the second floor and down the hall to their former jail.

The door was locked. "What's up with that?" asked Keoni.

"Do you think they would leave us locked-up with a tsunami coming?" asked Leilani.

Keoni ignored the question. "Let's go around back and see if the rope is still hanging out the window."

The twins flew down the stairs, raced through the kitchen, and out the back door. As they rounded the corner, the security lights lit up the backyard.

"Look, Lei, the rope's still there! They never even checked on us. I can't believe anyone would leave us locked-up on purpose!"

"Maybe they thought the tsunami would take care of us."

"That's cold. Really cold," said Keoni, shaking his head.

They made the ascent up the wall with ease and gazed in all directions from their perch at the top. As far as the eye could see there was *aa*—black, rough, sharp, hard lava. The house was built in the middle of an old lava flow, and there didn't appear to be any other houses nearby.

Directly beneath the wall, extending out at least six feet, was a hedge—a dense, untamed thicket of bougainvillea.

Forty-five

After all they'd been through, they were hemmed in on the edge of the sea with a tsunami coming.

Now what? Going over the wall was impossible. Braving fields of lava with its hidden crevices, barefoot, at night, with only the beam from the dive lights would be foolish. The odds of escaping unscathed were stacked against them. Climbing the electrified gate was out of the question too.

"We're stuck," murmured Leilani.

"Hey, let's go back to the house, fix something to eat, and watch the tsunami on TV," suggested Keoni, trying to sound upbeat. "Look, Sis, lots of times tsunamis don't hit. They fizzle out or miss the islands totally. And the tsunami scared Dr. Vile and his guys off. That's something to be thankful for."

"Yeah, and Johann should be safely out to sea by now," said Leilani.

They descended the wall and trudged back to the house. They made a pit stop in the well-equipped kitchen and raided the refrigerator, fixing themselves sandwiches and gorging on the leftover *pupu* from Dr. Vile's dinner party.

They stacked their plates high with food including pieces of dark chocolate cake with smooth, shiny frosting.

Leilani arranged their plates on the same tray the big man had used to serve them. Heading for Dr. Vile's abandoned inner sanctum, they could hear the TV on, just the way they'd left it.

"This is so weird," said Keoni, as they settled down in front of Dr. Vile's home theater.

Leilani nodded, too busy eating to speak.

As they ate and channel surfed, the twins began to feel better, and almost at home. A little *too* at home, perhaps.

As usual, Keoni had control of the remote.

"What is it about guys that you always have to have the remote?" said Leilani. "And the way you zip through the channels. How can you even tell what's on?

"Keoni, stop flipping through the channels! You're driving me crazy! Check out the news. See if there's anything on the tsunami."

"Huh? Oh. Right. Okay," said Keoni absently. He settled on Headline News but there were no updates.

"Maybe we should try the radio again," suggested Leilani. "You do that, okay, *Brah*? And I'll call the lagoon. Johann's probably gone by now but it won't hurt to check."

Keoni headed for the kitchen to search for news on the radio and retrieve another piece of chocolate cake. Leilani switched on the microphone and called out to Johann, not expecting an answer.

"Johann, Johann, are you there?"

"Leilani, you've got to get out, there's a big wave coming!

I can hear it," came the urgent reply. And even as Johann was issuing his warning, his voice was harmonious and comforting.

"Oh, Johann, it's so good to hear your voice again. But why haven't you gone yet? The cave, is it still open?"

"Yes, my dear. I was waiting to make sure all my friends were safe. Sonny is the only one here with me now."

Johann spoke to his friend. "You must leave at once!" he commanded, but Sonny stood fast.

Leilani could hear the devotion in little Sonny's tiny voice as he said, "I'll go when you go, Mr. Johann."

Leilani was aghast! "You've both got to get out of there! Sonny, please, talk to him, make him leave!"

Even though they had never met personally, Leilani had developed a soft spot in her heart for Sonny. There was something endearing about his loyalty to Johann and his high-pitched, miniature voice, defiant in the face of the gigantic mammal.

Leilani explained as quickly as she could why she and Keoni were still in the house. How Dr. Vile and his men had left them locked-up, or so their captors had thought, in the upstairs room to await their fate.

They were trapped and all they could do was hope and pray the tsunami turned out to be a dud.

It was then that Keoni ran into the room, his heart racing. "We're in deep doo-doo! The tsunami really is coming!" he shouted. "The biggest in fifty years!"

"Leilani, Keoni, listen to me," said Johann. "Come to the lagoon. You can leave with us."

"But how, Mr. Johann?" asked Keoni.' "The access to the beach is hidden and we don't know where it is."

"Let's give it a try, Keoni. They carried us through the hedge, maybe we can find the way out. Besides, what choice do we have?" said Leilani.

But Keoni had another concern. "How can we hold our breaths long enough to make it through the cave and to the surface?"

"Well, we made it when we got sucked through the first time."

"That happened at warp speed, Lei. I'm not sure we can get through the cave fast enough, even if we are with Johann. Hey, wait a minute! We can use the scuba gear! The fins may be too big but we can wear the BCD's, masks, and snorkels!"

"Mr. Johann, hold on, we'll be right back," Keoni yelled into the microphone and they took off down the hall.

Once again the twins found themselves in the scuba room. They could use the huge harness to hold onto Johann and strap the tanks to their backs. All they had to do was find the way through the bougainvillea barrier and lug the heavy canisters of air down to the water, and . . .

Keoni lifted one tank, then two, then the third. He hoisted the fourth, and then the last. The tanks were light enough to pick up with one hand.

"Empty, they're all empty! *Shoots!* What will we do now?"

Forty-six

The tsunami warning had everyone alarmed. Captain Kenny feared for his precious *Hana Hou*.

He had picked up Charlie on the way to the harbor immediately after the siren went off. The trusted first mate knew his responsibilities and was ready when the captain arrived unannounced at his door. They were to sail the *Hana Hou* out to sea, safely away from shore until the threat of the tsunami was *pau*.

If the *Hana Hou* remained in the harbor and the tsunami struck, she could end up looking like wooden matchsticks floating on the water, not the sleek and beautiful sailing vessel she was.

There was no hint of impending disaster in that balmy, cloudless night. Thousands of stars blinked in the sky like flakes of phosphorous in a dark sea. But a tsunami was coming.

Captain Kenny and Charlie pulled into a parking lot that was a safe distance from the harbor. The captain spotted what looked like Kalani's truck. "But what would he be doing here at this hour?" the captain wondered aloud.

The harbor was already abuzz with human activity, for

all the boats anchored there would be heading out to safety. Captain Kenny and Charlie sauntered toward the *Hana Hou,* pausing to *talk story* with their fellow boatmen. The subject, of course, was the tsunami. Their casual demeanor concealed the urgency they felt inside.

It wasn't the first time they'd been through this drill, but this looked like it could be the real thing. That had been a mighty powerful earthquake near Alaska.

Seeing Pua and Kalani on the dock, standing side-by-side with Kalani's arm around his wife's shoulders was as unexpected as the tsunami siren itself. "What are you guys doing here?" asked the captain, surprised but nonetheless pleased.

"We knew the *Hana Hou* would be in danger and we thought we'd come along for moral support," answered a weary but smiling Pua. She and Kalani were unable to sleep after hearing the siren. Their house was well away from the tsunami zone and they had nothing to fear.

"The truth is, we're worried to death about the kids. We couldn't just sit it out. I thought if we were together at least, out there . . . " Auntie Pua gestured weakly and looked toward the channel, tears forming in her eyes.

As Auntie Pua continued to speak, sadness crept into her voice. "Maybe there'll be a sign. Maybe Johann will turn up. We'd like to be with you on the *Hana Hou.* Kalani can help if you need an extra hand." She nodded toward Captain Kenny's broken arm, still encased in its fiberglass cast. With a cheerfulness in her voice that didn't fool anybody she added, "I make a great pot of coffee, and I brought *pupu* too."

It was then that Captain Kenny spied the *lauhala* basket

on Auntie Pua's arm, with glimpses of aluminum foil and plastic containers. Having sampled Auntie Pua's delicious food before, he smiled in remembrance.

"Welcome aboard," bellowed the captain, a little too heartily, as if he were greeting old friends he was taking on a pleasure cruise.

It wasn't easy for Auntie Pua to cross the narrow gangway to the deck of the bobbing vessel but she looked straight ahead and did not falter. She made her way below to stash her basket of goodies and Uncle Kalani started to help Charlie undo the lines.

Charlie was the first to see the shrouded figure hurrying down the dock toward them, arms waving in the air. A familiar voice called out, "Wait, wait!"

Charlie squinted, trying to identify the approaching caller, but the others knew immediately who it was. As quickly as her old legs could carry her, Mrs. Witherspoon hurried their way.

"Wait, wait!" she hollered again, "it's me, Clara."

Breathless, she reached the gangway. "May I join you?"

What could the captain say but, "welcome aboard," feeling guilty for not wanting Clara Witherspoon on the *Hana Hou,* especially at such a crucial time. He had been happy to see Kalani and Pua. Unfortunately he didn't feel the same way about Clara. Well, she'd better remember that he was captain of this ship.

Mrs. Witherspoon, sensing Captain Kenny's reluctance, felt the need to explain herself. "Our house is near the water, in the tsunami zone, so we had to be evacuated. Mr.

Witherspoon's gone to stay with friends up the hillside 'til this is over. I knew you'd have to take the *Hana Hou* out, and there's no telling how long it'll be. I thought an extra pair of eyes might be helpful, and I brought some snacks."

There was not much in the way of conversation as Charlie, Kalani and the captain went about their tasks, motoring out of the harbor and into the channel as they'd done a thousand times before. The women sat on the deck drinking coffee in the same spot the twins had sipped hot chocolate on that fateful morning.

They both started to talk at the same time. "You go first," said Auntie Pua deferring to the woman she thought of as her elder.

"No, that's okay, you first," replied Mrs. Witherspoon, sensing the need for Auntie Pua to unload her thoughts.

Before Auntie Pua spoke she took a long, deep breath and exhaled slowly, turning her head to look Mrs. Witherspoon gently in the eye. "Let's call a spade a spade, Clara. Maybe it's time to admit that maybe they're not coming back . . . "

Auntie Pua turned away and gazed out at the dark water, no longer able to face Mrs. Witherspoon without crying. Silently, the tears streamed down Auntie Pua's rosy cheeks. Her chest heaving, she was unable to speak further, lest she choke on her words.

Mrs. Witherspoon put her arm around Auntie Pua's shoulders and gave her a long, kind-hearted squeeze. Mrs. Witherspoon knew what her friend was feeling for she felt the same way, but with the added burden of enormous guilt.

Forty-seven

Johann was all business. "I'll come as close to shore as I can and wait for you," he announced, letting it be known by his tone that the matter was not open to debate. "I'll be singing. Call out my name in the direction of my voice and I'll find you."

"We're on our way," confirmed Leilani.

Like a swimming coach at a high-stakes meet, Johann encouraged his young friends. "Good luck. You can do it!" Conviction emanated from his voice, a welcome vote of confidence for Keoni and Leilani.

"We'll see you soon, Johann," said Keoni, ending the communication on an equally positive note, trying to believe his own words.

With masks and snorkels from the scuba room in hand, the twins didn't look back. They bolted out the kitchen door and ran across the lawn toward the sound of the high tide, dragging the harness behind them. There was no need to switch on the dive lights, for the security lights turned night into day, providing ample illumination.

Keoni and Leilani inspected the impenetrable wall of leafy

color and found nothing out of the ordinary, "Maybe there's something in the command post we missed," said Keoni.

"Oh, pleeeze, don't say that. I hate that house. I'll never go back."

Keoni carefully picked up a thorn-studded stick, and used it to move the branches aside for a more thorough inspection.

"This is it, Lei. We're at the end of the line," said Keoni turning to look at his sister with only a yard of hedge left to probe.

"Ah, Keoni . . . sorry about the shirt."

"No problem, Sis . . . and you know what? It looked really good on you."

Keoni moved aside the last stretch of dangling branches. His eyes widened, "Hello! What's this?"

Under the dense foliage was a large pot sitting on a plant trolley. A length of stout rope with a loop at one end served as a handle. Keoni and Leilani tightly clasped the rope handle and planted their bare feet firmly on the ground. They steeled themselves, focusing all their strength, and Leilani began the count that signaled the beginning of their tug-of-war.

"Ready—set—go!"

Once they got the trolley wheels rolling over the berm of dirt and rock, their obstinate foe gave up its post. It cooperated fully with its new masters, finally revealing the route of escape. Leilani and Keoni charged through the blessed opening, yanking the harness behind them. Led by the dive lights' narrow beams, they gingerly picked their way across slippery rocks toward the lapping surf.

The twins stood quietly at the water's edge, listening for a lone song in the vastness of their surroundings. Once they were still it wasn't difficult to hear Johann's stirring voice.

"Listen. Did you hear that?" Keoni asked. "Let's get wet."

They slipped on the adult-sized masks with the snorkels attached, tightening up the straps as best they could. Keoni shined his dive light on the shoreline, looking for a good spot to enter the dark water, its twinkling highlights courtesy of the moon.

"Keoni, what's that? Move the light back that way," instructed Leilani, directing her brother's arm. There in the crosshairs of their intersecting lights, bobbing among the rocks in the shallow water was a splash of yellow.

"Keoni, look! It's one of my fins!"

Leilani slowly made her way along the shoreline trying not to fall on the slippery, seaweed-covered rocks that surrounded the elusive fin. She made a grab for it and missed, the tide carrying it just out of reach as she made her move. Leilani didn't take her eyes off the prize as she waited patiently for its inevitable return, like a gecko stalking a moth under a porch light.

At just the right moment Leilani lunged. She seized the precious fin, teetering on the grassy rocks, her toes clenched around them. Though wobbly at first, she found her balance and stepped lightly to higher ground.

"One fin is better than no fin," said Leilani, hopping around on her left foot as she slipped the fin on her right. "I'll tell you what. I'll wear it and we can both hold on to the harness."

"I hope that harness isn't too much of a drag in the water. It could slow us down," mumbled Keoni. "But let's give it a shot anyway."

The Tuna Twins plunged into water the color of midnight, swimming toward Johann's voice. They called out in unison, "Johann, Johann, we're headed your way!"

Johann was daunting. When the twins first encountered him they nearly passed out from shock. They knew in theory he was enormous but to come face to face with the forty-ton leviathan was another story.

When the twins had suggested using the harness, Johann's initial reaction was "no way." He had his pride. Beasts of burden wore harnesses. And after all, the harness was what helped capture him in the first place.

But he quickly came to realize it was a practical idea. It would have been wildly romantic to flee together with the twins clinging to the small dorsal fin on his back. The reality was it would have been dangerous. The kids could easily get knocked off by a wave or choppy seas.

"So the harness it must be," relented Johann, getting over his indignation and chastising himself for this lapse into vanity. It was a great idea, maybe even a brilliant one.

Forty-eight

Sonny was exhausted. It was a struggle to keep up with the determined Johann, who had made a beeline for the twins. Before he knew it, Johann was out of sight, and Sonny found himself alone.

He could go no further. He heard Johann singing but didn't have the strength to follow his trail. The memory of the family that was no more came crashing back. He felt as deflated as a helium balloon that had been stuck with a pin.

He hung suspended in the water, not moving or whimpering, for he didn't have the energy for self-pity. Sonny became strangely detached. He felt no fear and waited for the end of his short life.

The spell was broken when a sudden tumult turned Sonny end over end, like a tumbleweed rolling in a desert wind.

"Sonny, meet the twins," the familiar voice roared in its excitement, forgetting how powerful it was, how it could blow little Sonny halfway across the lagoon.

This time, softly so as not to cause a ripple, Johann asked his friend, who was glowing like bright fish scales, "Sorry, partner, you okay?"

"Mr. Johann, you came back for me!" whispered little Sonny. A whisper was all he could muster.

"Of course. You didn't think I'd leave you, did you? Now, let's get out of here. We don't have much time. We've really gotta *hele* on!"

"Sorry, Mr. Johann, you must go on without me. I'll just slow you down," gasped Sonny, not wanting Johann or the twins to be endangered on his account. At least he could go to his watery grave knowing he had a friend who cared.

"Don't be silly," insisted Leilani, "you can ride along with us."

It was in that moment that Sonny first saw the twins, two masked look-a-likes, clinging to something that was strapped around Johann.

"Yeah, Sonny, you can ride in the pocket of my shorts," offered Keoni. "Swim on over here."

With renewed vigor, Sonny managed to propel himself toward the twins. Keoni tried to snatch the slippery Sonny as he floated past. He had his hand around the little squid's tiny body but Sonny squirted out like toothpaste from a tube.

"Come on, Sonny, you can do it," encouraged Keoni.

Sonny made another pass, getting a little closer to the bobbing Keoni who succeeded this time in holding on to him.

"Now Sonny, don't be scared. I'm going to put you in my pocket."

Sonny didn't resist, although his instinct told him to, and he overrode the urge to squirm from Keoni's grasp.

It's okay in here, not bad, he thought, poking his head

out of the top of Keoni's pocket. Keoni patted him reassuringly on the back. "We're all set here, Johann. Sonny's safe with us. Full steam ahead."

Forty-nine

"Whee-oo!" It was the thrill of a lifetime. No amusement park roller coaster could compare with this, gliding through the moonlit water leashed to Johann Sebastian Humpbach. With the twins in tow, Johann moved effortlessly across the surface, toward their escape hatch, the cave. Keoni and Leilani were able to forget for the moment the danger they faced. They reveled in the ride as they clung to Johann's side, weightless as astronauts in space.

Keoni rested one hand lightly on his pocket making sure Sonny didn't fall out. He remembered how distraught Johann had been when he had reached the twins and realized the little squid hadn't kept up with him. Fortunately, Johann was able to retrace his path through the water to where he had last seen his missing friend. Sonny had been like a lonely beacon in that now deserted lagoon, a glowing blue dot that drew his rescuers toward him.

The wild ride ended when they reached the lava fortress that had served as Johann's prison. The travelers hovered on the surface over the entrance to the cave. "I think it would be a good idea if you tread water while I check it out again," said Johann.

Johann dove to the cave's entrance. *Hmm, it's going to be a tight squeeze,* he thought. *They dragged me through it so I guess I'll fit going the other way.* Johann wished he knew how long the cave was. Once they were on that path they could not turn back. There was no room for a U-turn.

Johann surfaced without telling his companions about his misgivings. The sound of the tsunami was becoming louder. There wasn't a moment to spare.

"Hang on, *keiki*," ordered Johann, "we're outa here!"

With Keoni, Leilani, and Sonny at his side, Johann said, "Take a deep breath, everyone," and dove for the entrance to the cave. Without pausing, they entered the watery passageway.

The deep but narrow tunnel made speed impossible. Fortunately, the Tuna Twins were practiced divers and had strong lungs. They could hold their breaths for almost a minute. Keoni and Leilani flattened themselves against the giant's body to keep from scraping against the walls. It was agony, like being trapped in a coalmine.

Even with dive lights, only blackness was before them. There was no light at the end of the tunnel. It was nighttime in the undersea world too.

Ah, good, thought Johann, *I'm getting the hang of it.* He began to pick up speed. It would be over before long. With a little bit of luck, they'd soon be back where this all started, the mouth of the cave. They could be at the surface in a few seconds once they were out in the open.

Again the twins would ride tethered to Johann, far out

to sea, and away from the danger that plagued the shore. That part they were looking forward to.

Uh, oh! Johann returned to a crawl. The water in the cave was becoming shallower and shallower. It was receding! Before they could say Johann Sebastian Humpbach they found themselves at a dead stop, Johann's belly on the lava floor, and Keoni and Leilani dangling from his side.

Fifty

Keoni and Leilani dropped safely from the leash into the knee-deep water that surrounded the beached whale. Keoni removed Sonny from his pocket and released the grateful squid into the liquid.

Air, there was air! The twins ripped off their masks and snorkels. They could breathe! Their chests heaved as they filled their lungs with the precious gift of oxygen.

Keoni managed to ask, "Lei, you okay?"

"Yeah, you?"

"I'm okay," said Keoni, shining his dive light around them. Johann's huge bulk lay flat on the cave floor. "Johann, are you alright?"

"Please say something, Mr. Johann," chimed in Sonny.

Johann didn't answer right away. Without the support of the ocean around him he was feeling his weight for the first time. "I don't feel so good. Now I know what it must be like to have a sumo wrestler fall on top of you."

Keoni and Leilani were touched by Johann's selfless attempt at humor but were beyond cheering up. Shivering in the damp darkness, they submerged themselves in water up to their necks to stay warm. Leilani pressed her cheek to Johann's side and said, "You must be miserable, and there's nothing we can do to help you."

"This sucks," said Keoni. "Johann's stuck and we're gonna get nailed when the waves come rolling in—smashed against the walls or blasted back into the lagoon. "We're doomed any way you look at it!"

The gloomy prediction echoed around them, bouncing off the walls. "Doomed, doomed, doomed," spoke the cave.

"Just let me think for a minute . . . " said Johann. "When the water comes rumbling back it will be powerful, but at least it won't be as strong as the water above. Maybe I can ride it out. After all, I am forty tons."

He looked at the twins. "But you won't be able to hold on to the harness when the water comes rushing through. It'll snatch you away."

Keoni and Leilani remained still. The only sound a tinkle, the water drip—drip— dripping from the sides of the cave into the puddle below. They had no solution to this mess. It fell upon Johann to come up with something, or this little adventure was over.

Leilani broke the silence. "Keoni, do you remember how long Mr. Ishimoto said it took for a tsunami to hit after the ocean pulls back?"

"Hmm . . . twenty minutes?" said Keoni. It seemed like ages ago that they were in Mr. Ishimoto's science class. "Yeah, twenty minutes. I got it right on a test."

"I've got it!" bellowed Johann, and the cave repeated, "I've got it! I've got it! I've got it!"

“What, Johann, what?” exclaimed the twins.

“My mouth is huge. It’s big enough to hold both of you. I’ll scoop up a little water, just enough to submerge Sonny. No worries, I’m a baleen whale. I don’t have any teeth.”

The twins knew Johann was referring to the accordion-like folds that captured krill, plankton or small fish when he gulped huge mouthfuls of water. He would eat by removing the food from the baleen with his tongue and then swallow.

“And no worries, *keiki*, my throat is the size of a grapefruit so I won’t be swallowing *you* any time soon.”

“When I open my mouth wide, climb in. Put Sonny in your pocket. I don’t want any accidents.”

No one balked. Not Leilani, Keoni or Sonny. Though climbing into the mouth of a gargantuan sea creature was a scary thought—even if he was their friend. And *auwe*, the smell!

“All for one and one for all,” said Johann.

The behemoth’s huge jaws opened. Leilani and Keoni, with Sonny in his pocket, climbed up the harness and hoisted themselves onto Johann’s soft, cushion-like tongue. He closed his gaping mouth, sealing his passengers inside.

The raging water came closer and closer. Johann didn’t see it coming but could hear it roar. He tensed every muscle in his huge body. The water rushed at him and around him, swirling furiously. Johann held fast. He was buffeted from side to side, not feeling the cuts and scrapes as he banged into the cruel cave walls again and again.

The wave passed, a break in the action until the next roller was upon them. Like Houdini, Johann burst free, escaped from the cave, and swam out to sea.

He dove deep, just in time to miss the freight train barreling overhead.

Fifty-one

Softer than sunset, the sunrise with its pale silver glow tinged in coral-pink never ceased to amaze Captain Kenny. He stood by Uncle Kalani at the wheel of the *Hana Ho* and scanned the horizon with his spyglass.

Mrs. Witherspoon was chatting with Charlie, though they too were on alert.

"I'm going below to get the binoculars," called out Auntie Pua. When she returned to her seat near the bow she adjusted the binocular focus. Panning the vista, she felt small under the boundless sky, like an ant in a biosphere. "You have to keep it together," she told herself once again.

If there was a tsunami rolling below no one on board the *Hana Hou* detected anything out of the ordinary. Auntie Pua was about to give Mrs. Witherspoon a turn with the binoculars when she thought she saw something familiar. It looked like a whale.

"Captain, did you see that!" Auntie Pua shouted with the excitement of a tourist seeing a whale for the very first time. "There's something there, at eleven o'clock!"

They watched and waited.

"There, there it is again!" screamed Auntie Pua, "Do you see it!"

"I think so. I think it *is* a whale. Yes, I see the spray!"

"Oh, please, God, let it be Johann," prayed Auntie Pua out loud.

"Now, we all have to stay calm. It's possible that other whales could be here now, you know," said the captain.

The whale appeared to change direction and head their way. "Lower the sails and drop anchor," ordered Captain Kenny. It was illegal to sail toward the endangered species and approach it closer than one hundred yards. If a whale came to you, that was a different matter.

Auntie Pua, her gaze fixed on the approaching creature, saw it vanish beneath the waves. The mariners held vigil, waiting, hoping for another sighting.

Out of the blue, the graceful back of a humpback whale broke the surface of the water just a few feet away from the anchored *Hana Hou*.

"Look, it's beside the boat!" they cried out.

"It's under the boat!"

"It's on the other side!"

It was so close there was no mistaking its identity. "It's Johann! It's Johann!" they shouted, recognizing his distinctive white tail flukes. "He's alive!"

His enormous head rose from the water like a rocket. "What's that weird contraption strapped around him?" cried Mrs. Witherspoon.

"It's some kind of harness!" the captain exclaimed.

Johann settled down after this splashy greeting, for

it must have given his passengers quite a jolt. Slowly he opened his massive jaws, and the twins saw the sunrise as they bobbed among the waves.

Fifty-two

"Oh my God! Oh my God! Somebody pinch me! Tell me I'm not dreaming!" Auntie Pua's spirit soared as the twins climbed up the familiar rope ladder and into her outstretched arms.

To the great whale she said, "Bless you, Johann. Bless you," She blew him a kiss and he responded with a little ditty before swimming away with Sonny tucked securely under his flipper,

It's been quite a ride
But we're okay
Just happy to see
Another day

Auntie Pua felt as light as the sky. As for Uncle Kalani, pure joy welled up inside, a feeling tender and strong. Auntie Pua and Uncle Kalani encircled the twins with hugs and laughter. Though lightheaded and dizzy, Keoni and Leilani basked in the love that surrounded them. Questions came from all directions, but there would be time for the answers later. Now was the time for tears.

The *Hana Hou's* exile at sea did not last long after the

twins were found.

"It's safe to return to the harbor," announced Captain Kenny, receiving the news on the *Hana Hou's* radio. "They said the tsunami struck with the predicted force, but mercifully bypassed the populated areas. It only hit the old lava fields on the southeastern part of the island. There aren't many houses out there. It appears there was no loss of life and only one structure was destroyed."

Captain Kenny started to steer the *Hana Hou* in the direction of the harbor when some debris came floating by. Leilani thought she saw what looked like a tall lamp.

The media was back in full force even before the Johann Sebastian Humpbach Whale Song Tour began. Johann had been tempted to postpone the tour after his ordeal, but reconsidered. "You can't disappoint your fans," Sonny told him.

Visitors from around the world jammed the island. There wasn't a room to be had. Nearly everyone wore a Johann T-shirt of one kind or another. Music companies and researchers readied their undersea recording equipment. Snorkelers, divers, surfers, and submariners bounced in the waves.

Johann began his concert by singing his own kind of music, a haunting whale song of old, echoing through undersea canyons and caves, reverberating through the now friendly seas. He sang Hawaiian *mele* too, songs old and new, some ballads, and even an old Hawaiian chant. Friends played with him on their *ukuleles* and guitars. He sang on the eastern side of the island, the white curtain of a waterfall behind him. He sang on the south shore, with the shrill voices of sea birds overhead. He sang arias for opera lovers and lightened the mood with a touch of pop.

The twins and their *ohana* on board the *Hana Hou* followed Johann from place to place, not missing a note. Together again, they basked in the joy and passion of Johann's music.

He sang an original composition for the twins, praising their courage and stalwart hearts. And he sang for Sonny.

The newspapers reported the concert as "triumphant." Johann was quoted as saying, "I am exhausted but happy."

Mrs. Witherspoon's well-planned official welcome had gone off without a hitch. Mr. Witherspoon was elated to present Johann with his *kukui nut lei* after all.

Captain Kenny went back to tending his boating business, though not without interruption from a zealous media. This time though, the captain and Mrs. Witherspoon managed to take some pleasure in their notoriety. The publicity resulted in reservations for the *Hana Hou* months in advance, and Mrs. Witherspoon enjoyed holding court on many a talk show.

After the tour, Sonny returned to his friends the reef dwellers and his home in the lagoon. The tsunami had blown apart Dr. Vile's monster wall so Johann would be able to visit Sonny any time he was in Hawaii.

As for Dr. Vile, he'd been spotted at the heliport with his cronies when a fight broke out among them. According to one account there was some pushing and shoving. An unidentified helicopter took off and one of the men, a big man, was left behind.

The police reported there had been a falling out because the big man objected to leaving the twins in harm's way. Dr.

Vile was in a foul mood, his well laid plans having gone awry and his losses enormous. He became enraged when one of his men dared to question his authority and a scuffle ensued. The big man was knocked unconscious on the tarmac.

When he came to, the dissident henchman told the police about Dr. Vile's house and the kids being locked-up there, but the authorities were powerless to do anything. The tsunami had already struck that part of the island. By the time the worst was over, the police found the house gone, demolished by the raging sea.

The newspapers reported Dr. Vile's whereabouts as still unknown.

After Keoni and Leilani had time to ponder everything that happened, they got to thinking about the big man's last-minute change of heart. "It must have been him who fixed up your cuts and stuff. And what about the chicken *katsu*? He had to go to town to get it. *Shoots*, there was plenty of other stuff in the fridge to eat," said Keoni.

"Do you think he thought local food would make us feel better?" Leilani wondered.

"Who knows? I guess he wasn't all bad."

Johann had mixed feelings about the scarf. On one hand, it had been a gift from that repulsive Dr. Vile. On the other hand, it was a thing of beauty. Someone's talented hands had made it. "If it weren't for the scarf the twins would never have gone through their ordeal," said Johann. "But I would not have made it out of the lagoon alive either.

"Please give the scarf to Keoni and Leilani for safekeeping," he requested of Mrs. Witherspoon, who was happy to be entrusted with the job.

"Hmm . . . these stars sparkle just like the candles on our birthday cake," said Keoni, examining the precious memento under the bright light of his desk lamp.

"So, *Sistah* . . . what'd you wish for anyway?"

"Ahhh . . . to meet Johann, B*rah*."

"Yeah? Me too."

HAWAIIAN PRONUNCIATION GUIDE

The Hawaiian language has 13 letters, including 5 vowels and 8 consonants.

Vowels are pronounced the same as in Spanish:

A=ah
E=a as in hay
I=e as in bee
O=o as in oh
U=u as in you

Consonants are pronounced as in English (h,k,l,m,n,p,w)

The okina (‘) is a glottal stop which means there is a break in a word, a sort of "catch" in your throat between the two parts of a word.

A "w" in the middle of a word is sometimes pronounced "v" as in Hawai'i. Hawai'i is commonly pronounced with a "w" sound but the "v" sound is more correct.

If two of the same vowels are side by side in a word you pronounce them both as in "aa" (ah ah). "Ai" is pronounced "eye" as in Lahaina. "Au" is pronounced "ow" as in Maui.

There is no "s" in Hawaiian. Singular and plural are the same.

Words You Might Not Know

Words are Hawaiian unless otherwise noted.

About Pidgin: When the people of different nationalities (Chinese, Japanese, Filipino, Portuguese) immigrated to Hawaii to work on the sugar plantations many years ago they needed a way to communicate with one another. Therefore they developed a simplified form of English which they mixed with other languages. This is known as Pidgin.

Also please note: There is no letter 's' in the Hawaiian language; singular and plural are expressed the same.

aa—stoney, rough, sharp type of lava

ahi—Hawaiian tuna fishes

aina—the land

auwe—oh!

akamai—smart, clever

aloha—hello, goodbye, love, affection, compassion, grace, kindness

aumakua—spirits of ancestors who have assumed the shape of various animals i.e. sharks, octopuses, owls and communicate in dreams and visions

haupia—pudding made of coconut creme; cake made with coconut creme

brah—(Pidgin) brother

buggah—(Pidgin) "bugger"

grinds—(Pidgin) food

Haleakala—House of the Sun; name of the dormant volcano that makes up the largest side of the island of Maui

hana hou—to do again, encore; name of Captain Kenny's boat

hele—to go, to move on

honu— sea turtle

howzit—(Pidgin) how's it going, how are you?

hula— graceful Hawaiian dance

humuhumunukunukuapua'a—Hawaiian trigger fish; the state fish

imu—underground oven

kalua—baked in an underground oven with Hawaiian salt

katsu—(Japanese) dish of chicken, fish or pork breaded and fried, served with a special sauce

keiki—child or children

kiawe—acacia tree

koa—native Hawaiian hardwood

kokua—help

Kona—southwest area of the Big Island of Hawaii; wind from the southwest

kukui—candlenut tree, has many uses, i.e., lei, medicines, oil used to fuel lamps and torches

kupuna—grandparent, ancestor, or close friend of grandparent's generation

lauhala—pandanus leaf, used in weaving bags, mats, hats and ornaments

lei—necklace of flowers, leaves, nuts, seeds or shells

lolo—crazy

luau—Hawaiian feast

Maui—one of the Hawaiian Islands, named for the demigod Maui

mahalo—thank you

maile—shiny, fragrant leaves found in the forest, used in making lei for special occasions

mele—song

Menehune—legendary race of little people who worked at night building roads, fish ponds and temples.

mauka—the area between where you are at any given moment and the mountains

muumuu—a loose fitting dress in a colorful Hawaiian print

nada—(Spanish) nothing

nalu—wave; name of Uncle Kawika's band

ohana—family; extended family

ono—delicious

opihi—limpet, type of shellfish

opu—tummy

pahoehoe—smooth, unbroken type of lava

pahoku—rock

pali—cliff

pareo—sarong, wraparound

pau—finished

Pavarotti, Luciano—(1935-2007) Italian operatic singer, the greatest and most successful tenor of his generation. Beloved world-wide, he was a giant of popular culture who crossed over into pop music. Known for his expansive personality, charm and considerable girth.

pilikia—trouble

plate lunch—(Pidgin) meat, chicken or fish served with "two scoops rice" and macaroni salad

poi—Hawaiian staff of life or staple pounded from the root of the taro (*kalo*) plant and thinned with water

pua—flower, blossom; name of the twins' auntie (Pua)

puka—hole

pupu—appetizer, hors d'ouevre

sushi—(Japanese) Bite-sized delicacy made with rice often combined with raw fish or vegetables and wrapped in nori; served with soy sauce, wasabi (hot radish paste), and pickled ginger

shaka—(Pidgin) hand signal meaning "hang loose," made with thumb and little finger extended and three middle fingers folded into the palm of the hand

shave ice—Hawaiian version of a snow cone with the ice "shaved" instead of crushed

shoyu—(Japanese) soy sauce

sistah—(Pidgin) sister

slippahs—(Pidgin) rubber slippers, flip-flops

talk story—(Pidgin) chit-chat, "shooting the breeze"

ti— colorful plant with long, narrow leaves and slender stem thought to bring good luck; used by Hawaiians for thatch, food wrappers, hula skirts and sandals

tutu—grandma, grandpa, grand uncle or aunt; any relative of grandparent's generation

upcountry—rural area on the slopes of the mountain Haleakala

wikiwiki—fast, speedy

Acknowledgements

I am indebted to Steven Goldsberry for getting me off on the right foot, or should I say five orange arms?

To Kathleen Ageton, Children's Librarian at the Kihei library, mahalo for your kokua. To Diane Nakoa, teacher par excellance, mahalo for your enthusiasm and encouragement. And to Kelly Dukelow, mahalo for entrusting your classes to me. Through them Johann was born.

As for the "mystery" student, wherever you may be, it was your dare that started it all and I thank you.

To Larry Yoder for encouraging, advising and going to bat for me, I thank you for your generous nature.

To super artist Kim Toft, mahalo for your inspiration.

My gratitude goes to Joletta Griswold and Sinthia Szato who embraced Johann with their unbridled encouragement and support; to Amy Novesky for helping me reach the next level and to Marilyn Donahue for going above and beyond my expectations. Mahalo, Joan Hansen, for making precious time for me. My sincere gratitude goes to Marsha Rogers for reminding me to "never quit before the miracle," and to Alana Kay for her unwavering optimism.

To readers Irene Bowie, Rik Fitch, Barbara Kaneshige,

and Dorothy Romson, mahalo for your encouragement and kind words.

To the Elwell family: sister Jackie, brother-in-law Lee, nephews Chris, Jonathan, and Danny, and my cousin Anita Joseph, your support, encouragement and insights have meant the world to me.

Mahalo nui loa to The Maui Writer's Conference for creating a smorgasbord for storytellers.

And to my husband Ralph, my rock, who cares for me like no other.

ABOUT THE AUTHOR

Jamie David is a writer, artist and former teacher living on the island of Maui. Born and raised in small town Pennsylvania, Jamie moved west after college and settled in San Francisco at an exciting time in the life of the city. The westward migration continued in 1986 when she and her husband Ralph made the move to Hawaii.

"Why can't we read something fun?" was the frequent refrain from her middle grade English students. A story set in Hawaii would grab their interest. It must be entertaining and informative too. *Shoots*! A search found nothing that fit the bill. Thus, *Johann Sebastian Humpbach* was born, inspired by and dedicated to Hawaii's keiki.

ORDER FORM

To order additional copies of Johann Sebastian Humpbach, please send a check made payable to Jamie David at:

Chai Yo Maui Press
P.O. Box 331
Kihei, HI 96753

	Price	Quantity	Subtotal
Johann Sebastian Humpach	$14.95		
Shipping and Handling	$4.00		
Additional Postage and Handling for each additional book	$1.00		
Sales Tax (Hawaii residents add 4%)			
Total			

Do you have a large order? Please call for quote.

MAILING INFORMATION

Name:

Address:

City: State: Zip:

If you wish to place a credit card order please visit our website at <www.johannsebastianhumpbach.com>.

Questions? Call (808) 205-7225.